"I hear you're looking f...
Will you stop me before I stop you?"

Charlotte's world narrowed to the interior of her car. The serial killer she'd been chasing for years was seated only feet away.

"I never stopped looking for you," she said.

But at the end of her statement, a quick prick nipped her neck. Had he pierced her with a needle? *Get out of the car. Now.* She pawed at the door handle but couldn't coordinate her fingers to take hold and pull. Her wild gaze traveled the parking lot, searching for anyone nearby who could come to her aid. The parking lot appeared empty of people. Black dots floated in her vision. She'd been drugged. Dizziness struck next. *I have to escape and find help.*

"Rest now," the voice whispered in her ear. "All I want is to talk. I promise."

She struggled to make sense of his words inside her slushy brain. The space around her grew smaller and darker. Her battle was lost. At least for right now. If she awoke—no, *when* she awoke—she'd fight.

Death at the hands of this man wasn't an option. Detective Charlotte Reid would not become another victim of the Presque Killer.

Multiple award-winning author **Laurie Winter** is a true warrior of the heart. Inspired by her dreams, she creates authentic characters who overcome the odds and find true love. She enjoys time with her family, who are scattered between Wisconsin and Michigan. Laurie has three kids and one fantastic husband, all who inspire her to chase her dreams.

Books by Laurie Winter

Love Inspired Suspense

Hunted by a Killer

Love Inspired The Protectors

Safeguarding the Witness

Visit the Author Profile page at LoveInspired.com.

Hunted by a Killer

LAURIE WINTER

LOVE INSPIRED SUSPENSE

INSPIRATIONAL ROMANCE

LOVE INSPIRED® SUSPENSE
INSPIRATIONAL ROMANCE

ISBN-13: 978-1-335-98006-9

Hunted by a Killer

Copyright © 2024 by Laurie Hoffman

Recycling programs for this product may not exist in your area.

For questions and comments about the quality of this book, please contact us at CustomerService@Harlequin.com.

® is a trademark of Harlequin Enterprises ULC.

Love Inspired
22 Adelaide St. West, 41st Floor
Toronto, Ontario M5H 4E3, Canada
www.LoveInspired.com

Printed in Lithuania

MIX
Paper | Supporting responsible forestry
FSC® C021394

Forbearing one another, and forgiving one another,
if any man have a quarrel against any:
even as Christ forgave you, so also do ye.
—*Colossians* 3:13

Dedicated to the CASA organization and the children I've been privileged to advocate for during my years as a volunteer. You are greater than your circumstances. You are a blessing to everyone in your life. You are my inspiration.

ONE

He's back. Her blood ran ice-cold, producing a shiver. Detective Charlotte Reid glanced down at the crime scene photo before sliding it back across the table to Chief Gunther. The last time she'd seen a body like that—a body drained of life and stripped of all human dignity—it had been her sister's. "It's the same killer. I'm sure." They'd never caught him. A failure that haunted Charlotte.

Chief Gunther rubbed a hand down his stubble-covered face. "I thought we put the dark days of brutal killings behind us. Things have been quiet in Presque for six years."

She'd never shared the chief's optimism. Her hometown of Presque, Louisiana, had been a sleepy Southern town until a serial killer had turned it into his hunting and dumping grounds. Four murdered women had been tied to one killer, with her younger sister, Ruby, as his last victim. Until yesterday, when he'd added one more to the list. The evidence confirmed what she suspected.

Last night after dinner, Charlotte had been notified a body was discovered. She didn't mind working long hours with no breaks. She had no family at home. No significant other who needed attention. She *did* mind being called out to a homicide and viewing the body of an innocent woman who would never spend another day with the ones she loved. Anger brewed in her stomach. She would not allow the cases to grow cold again.

She continued her update to the police chief. "Our most recent victim has ligature marks on her neck. Red fibers were found embedded in her skin. She was left in a ditch outside of town." Charlotte's sister had been posed in an identical manner. "Most significantly, there's a crescent moon shape carved into her inner upper arm." The mark of a killer who wanted his murders linked. Did he believe he was too smart to be caught? To date, he *had* been.

"The crime lab needs to complete its testing. Could be a copycat." The chief pushed up to his feet. Collecting the crime scene photographs, he placed them into a large envelope. "But I already alerted the FBI under the presumption we're dealing with the same perpetrator. They're sending an agent to assist. He should be here soon."

"Soon? The body was discovered last night. Surely the FBI won't send anyone down yet. And why not wait for assistance until we know what we're dealing with?" Having federal assistance meant she'd have access to resources outside her department's reach…but it also meant an FBI suit with a badge would take over her investigation. She checked her ego, refusing to let pride overpower good judgment. Last time, she'd waited too long to trust her federal partner and risked the quality of the investigation.

Charlotte had to remain on this case. The Presque Police Department wasn't large and lacked the resources of its big city counterparts. If she stepped aside, the Kingston Parish Sheriff's Department would likely take over the investigation. The department's prior work on the murder investigations left her uneasy about handing over a case of such great importance. It hadn't prioritized solving the killings of drug-addicted girls. Charlotte had to catch the sick per-

son who killed vulnerable women—including her *sister*—
and had gotten away with it for too long. That meant she
needed the help federal law enforcement offered, and she
couldn't allow her personal feelings to obstruct her work.
Not like last time. Her former partnership with Special
Agent Austin Walsh had been a distraction. Or should she
say her emotional and physical attraction to the man had
caused her to lose focus. A mistake that had contributed to
the cases going cold. Her love for her late sister and drive
to catch Ruby's killer surpassed any dreams of romance.
Nothing could stand in her way.

*Don't assume the FBI will send Austin again—even if
his working knowledge of these cases makes him the most
logical option.*

"The feds deploy their resources rapidly. Detective, you
know better than anyone that waiting to call in the feds
could mean another murder." Chief Gunther placed the
folder into her hands. The phone on his desk rang, and he
glanced over to check the caller ID. "I need to take this.
The FBI agent has your contact information and will reach
out when he arrives."

She closed her eyes, willing the strength to see this case
to the end. *Please God, don't let me falter.*

"Charlotte." The chief rested a hand on her shoulder.
"If you can't handle facing these murders again, speak up.
I can assign…"

"I can handle it." She didn't let him finish. "I have to
stop this madman and bring my sister's killer to justice."
The note found on the ground near the latest victim left no
doubt of his intentions.

*"I've tried to be good but the urge to kill won't leave
me. Can you find me before I find you?"*

When she'd arrived at the scene last night to find the

note left with the victim, she knew the Presque Killer had returned. If he sought attention, he had it. He would find no safe harbor in the town of Presque. She would flush him out before he hurt another soul.

Special Agent Austin Walsh had taken an early morning flight from Reagan National to Baton Rouge then headed straight to Presque, about a forty-five-minute drive.

He turned onto the main road, in the direction of the police station. The charm of the small town remained since his last visit. He passed a white clapboard-sided church topped by a tall steeple and wide front doors. A stain remained about three feet up the exterior wall, indicating where the water had stopped rising after the last hurricane swept through. A few stately homes lined the street like old sentinels, dripping with Southern architecture and history. He found the downtown area quiet, and the remaining stores still in business showed off attractive window displays. A colorful banner for the town's annual jazz festival draped high over the street. Unfortunately, a darkness stained the underbelly of the area. Five women had been brutally murdered, and their killer was still at large. Austin had failed last time to arrest the person responsible. He wouldn't make the same mistake again.

Six years ago, he'd worked in Presque and the surrounding area for six months with no answers. Three women had been murdered in similar manners in the year prior to his assignment to the case. Charlotte's sister had been the fourth, found murdered two months after he'd arrived in Presque. The trace DNA evidence collected on the first known victim's shirt offered no match to anyone in the system. Other than the drop of DNA, the killer had been clean in conducting his crimes. With no solid leads in four months after Charlotte's sister's murder, he was called back to his home office and forced to admit failure to his mentor—someone who understood losing a loved one to the hands of a serial killer.

His recollection of those events brought Charlotte's pretty face to mind. An attraction to the local detective had been one of those mistakes he planned to avoid during this visit.

He parked, then scanned the case briefing one more time. The truth was, he'd memorized the facts of the old cases. They never were far from his mind, despite the many other investigations he'd closed since. His background with this community and the victims was the reason he'd been brought back. But the prospect of going into the Presque Police Station and facing Detective Charlotte Reid after six years kept him glued to the seat of his rental.

You're stalling. Austin gathered up his nerve and exited the vehicle. Lifting his chin, he strode to the station's front door. He introduced himself to the man posted at the lobby window, then waited to be taken back to the police chief.

The door to the lobby opened and Chief Alan Gunther appeared. "Special Agent Walsh." He held out a hand in greeting. "Welcome back."

Austin was back, but for how long? Would he hit the same walls as before? He shook the offered hand and followed the chief down a brightly lit hallway and into his office. "Any leads?"

"None yet. Detective Reid is heading back to the scene to make sure nothing was overlooked." Chief Gunther leaned on the front of his desk. His left foot tapped on the tile floor.

Austin remained standing as well. A supercharged energy flowed through him. He was eager to get started. "I'll head over with her." He paused, considering his words. "In your opinion, can Detective Reid handle this investigation?

If the killer we're chasing is the same person who murdered her sister, she could be too close to the case. Who else is available to take over if needed?"

He thought back to the last time he'd worked with Charlotte. She was the best local detective he'd ever teamed up with. A few years out of the FBI Academy, he'd been assigned to investigate a string of similar murders, starting with women disappearing in the Baton Rouge area then finally culminating in Presque. Detective Reid had led the latter investigation until her sister went missing. Then her sister had become a murder victim. They'd tried to convince Charlotte to step down but the woman dug in. She'd refused to give up the hunt. In the end, Austin had left town with an unfulfilled mission and a local law enforcement partner he'd let down.

He'd failed so many, including Charlotte. An outcome he wouldn't repeat. The Presque cases were dark spots on his career with the FBI, which had been filled with mostly captured murderers and accolades. Though Special Agent Caleb Boyce had died three months ago, Austin vowed to continue Caleb's important work of studying, hunting and catching serial killers. Austin wished to carry on the legacy of the man who'd been his instructor at the FBI Academy, an invaluable mentor and a trusted friend. Caleb had worked tirelessly to bring his daughter's murderer to justice. Austin could help bring peace to the families of the Presque Killer's victims.

Chief Gunther folded his arms and released a breath. "You know how I feel about our parish sheriff's department getting involved any more than they have to. Remember how badly they bungled the investigation the last time they got involved? Here's the thing." He paused and looked Austin straight in the eye. "I'm not placing Detective Reid on the sidelines without cause. She is the most committed detective I have to solve these murders."

That was what worried him. He'd witnessed fellow FBI agents grind themselves down to dust while working a case, including Caleb. Charlotte had been close to losing herself after her sister's murder. If she remained on the case, he'd keep a close eye on her. "I trust your judgment," he replied to the chief.

"Go see if you can catch Detective Reid before she leaves," Chief Gunther said. "I expect a report on the progress of the investigation by the end of the day."

He nodded, familiar with complying with orders from the local chief of police. Not that he was obligated to. He'd learned that to keep the peace, if the order didn't go against the direction of his own work, he'd cooperate. If the local law enforcement got in his way, he issued a reminder of who he answered to.

Austin stepped out of the chief's office and made his way to the section of the station where Charlotte's desk was located. Or at least had been. When he caught sight of her at her desk, head down in concentration, he paused. Besides longer hair, she looked the same.

The charge of fascination he felt proved he hadn't gotten over her. He'd have to—immediately. Their relationship was strictly professional. Austin had come to do a job: put a killer behind bars.

Charlotte sat at her desk, gathering the files she needed before leaving for the crime scene. At the sound of footsteps, she raised her gaze. Her chest squeezed at the sight of Austin Walsh striding toward her. She hadn't wanted to see him again under these conditions.

Then again, under what other circumstances would their

paths have crossed again? He was an FBI special agent who investigated serial homicides. She was a small-town detective. Working murder cases was not conducive to forming healthy relationships, even a friendship. And they hadn't been friends the last time she'd been this close to him. When he declared he'd been taken off the case and recalled to his home office, she'd taken out her frustration on him. She'd yelled and attempted to bully him into staying, and in the end she couldn't bring herself to say goodbye. Her shame at the way she'd conducted herself had recessed over time. But seeing him again brought all the feelings rushing back. Austin hadn't fought to remain on the Presque cases, which had grown cold. The two of them had failed to complete their job, and that knowledge haunted her every day since he'd left.

"Hello." She kept her greeting cool and professional. Standing, she offered a hand.

"Hi." He shook her hand. "It's been a while. How have you been?"

She quickly pulled her hand out of his grasp. "I'll be better when a murderer isn't walking the streets."

"I second that." He set the messenger bag he'd been carrying onto the empty office chair next to her desk. "I was told you're leading the recent investigation and believe the Presque Killer is responsible."

Austin's black dress slacks and button-down shirt advertised he wasn't local law enforcement. His styled hair, face perfectly made for a classic movie screen, and crisp attire suited his personality—all cool confidence and swagger. In her opinion, he deserved every ounce of ego he'd accumulated. Austin excelled at his job. He was precise and reserved. He'd brought down several high-profile serial killers and other criminals since they'd last worked together. According to the articles she'd read about some of his solved cases, Austin was a rising star—one of the top serial killer specialists in the Bureau. She'd seen him in action and been impressed by his sharp mind and accurate instincts.

She broke eye contact and returned to organizing the files of prior case notes. "Whoever murdered the woman we found last night is either the Presque Killer or a superior copycat. We're still waiting on lab test results but my gut tells me it's him."

"Okay, then, let's get to work." He rubbed his hands together. "Chief mentioned you're heading back to the crime scene for another look."

"I was preparing to leave right before you arrived. You're welcome to join me." The invitation had caught in her throat but her training overrode her awkward need to get far away from him.

"Sure. We can ride together."

"I have some other business to attend to afterward. We'll ride separately." A concocted excuse. She doubted she'd be able to avoid being in a car together forever.

"Understood. I'll follow you." He grabbed his bag.

"I'm parked out back. Watch for a silver sedan. I'll swing around the building and drive past. The scene is approximately two miles west of the town limits." She waited for him to leave her desk area before taking a deep breath. *You can do this. No hard feelings. You're working together toward a common goal. That's all.*

With the folder of investigative materials in her hand, she strode around a barricade wall and across a long stretch of pavement to her car, which the vehicle maintenance staff had neglected to lock after bringing it back from the maintenance shop. She got in, then turned on the vehicle to start the AC. In this heat, she only needed seconds before her shirt began sticking to her sweat-covered skin. Could she trade Louisiana humidity for snow? Cold weather was preferable for preserving a crime scene.

The body had been found at dusk in a swampy ditch on the side of the gravel road outside of town. Charlotte had walked the scene soon after the call came in but wanted a chance to reexamine it with fresh eyes in the daylight. Like the previous times, the killer had left his victim near the roadside, as if he wanted them to be found before wild animals destroyed his work. A group of high school boys out cruising the country roads had discovered the body. The preliminary report estimated she'd died approximately eighteen hours prior. The young woman hadn't been identified yet. Photographs and her basic information were uploaded into the federal missing persons system. No match yet. Perhaps she hadn't been missing long enough for someone to notice. Or perhaps she hadn't had anyone in her life who missed her. Like the other victims, another vulnerable girl stolen off the streets. The assumption brought tears to her eyes.

Charlotte hadn't reported Ruby missing until the day after she'd disappeared. She'd been wrapped up in work and when she learned her sister hadn't come home, she assumed Ruby had broken her vow of sobriety and stayed out partying. Looking back, as a detective investigating a serial killer, she should have known better. After searching every hole she'd known her sister to frequent, she'd feared for Ruby more than any other time in her life. Two days later, a local farmer had found Ruby's body. Her sister had been dumped like a bag of trash. A final indignity that Charlotte would never forgive. Ruby hadn't been perfect. She'd endured the trauma of parental abandonment, along with Charlotte. While Charlotte had been able to break free and build a successful life, Ruby had found comfort in bad relationships, drugs and alcohol.

Charlotte had to focus on the case before her. Dwelling on her sorrow over losing Ruby wouldn't help her catch the killer. She gripped the steering wheel, willing herself into the present, and took long, deep breaths. The Presque Killer would not slip away. Not again.

She took hold of the transmission lever to put the car into Reverse. The moment her finger touched the lever, she froze at the sensation of metal on the side of her neck. "Who's there?"

A quiet laugh answered.

She shifted forward in her seat and glanced in the rear-view window to try to glimpse the person behind her. "Answer me."

The man's breathing grew louder. "I hear you're looking for me again. Will you stop me before I stop you?"

His voice sounded digital and strange. Charlotte's world narrowed to the interior of her car. The serial killer she'd been chasing for years could be seated only feet away. "I never stopped looking for you." With the end of her statement, a quick prick nipped her neck. Had he pierced her with a needle? *Get out of the car, now.* She pawed at the door handle but couldn't coordinate her fingers to take hold and pull. Her wild gaze traveled her surroundings, searching for anyone nearby who could come to her aid. The parking lot appeared empty of people. Black dots floated in her vision. She'd been drugged. Dizziness struck next. *I have to escape and find help.*

"Rest now," the voice whispered in her ear. "All I want is to talk, I promise."

Talk? She struggled to make sense of his words inside her slushy brain. A serial killer had drugged her and all he wanted to do was talk? Images of her sister floated into her mind. Death at the hands of this man wasn't an option. She flung herself toward the car door and desperately tried to get out. The space around her grew smaller and darker. Her battle was lost. At least for right now. If she awoke— no, when she awoke—she'd fight.

Detective Charlotte Reid would *not* become another victim of the Presque Killer.

TWO

A uniformed police officer rapped her knuckles on the passenger-side window of Austin's car.

Startled, Austin jumped in his seat, then lowered the car window.

"Are you waiting for Detective Reid?" the officer asked.

"She asked I wait for her to drive by then follow her to the crime scene." Had he missed her? He glanced in the rearview mirror before checking the time. He'd been waiting for ten minutes. What was taking so long?

"I saw her car drive away not that long ago. It was going fast and heading east, in the opposite direction of where they found the body." She glanced back at the front door of the police station. "Chief Gunther noticed you were sitting out here and asked me to check in."

He turned off the car engine and exited the vehicle. "Has anyone tried contacting her?"

"No, but I'll call her cell now." The officer dialed and waited. "It went to voice mail." She attempted twice more to get through. "Detective Reid isn't answering."

"Something's not right." Probably nothing to panic over. Still, he carried an uncomfortable weight of worry in his gut. Detective Reid's negative feelings for him might remain, but Austin trusted her professionalism. He understood how seriously she took her work on this case.

He strode to the parking lot behind the station and walked the perimeter, then crisscrossed the area, searching for anything out of place. Austin still had Charlotte's cell phone number saved in his contacts. He dialed, and as ringing sounded, he prayed she'd answer.

The sound of a cell phone chime caught his attention. He followed the noise until it stopped, which coincided with his call going to voice mail. He dialed Charlotte again—and once again the chiming started. Lying in the mulch under a bush at the edge of the lot was a black cell phone. On the cracked screen, his name displayed as the caller. He pressed End on his call.

What had happened, and where was Charlotte?

A possibility left him cold. If a serial killer had resumed his hunt, had he just taken his next victim? Detective Reid might be perfectly safe but as a federal special agent trained to hunt serial criminals, specifically murderers, Austin didn't trust in optimism.

Pushing down fear, he steadied his emotions. He'd left his evidence collection kit in his messenger bag, which was in the car. Be Prepared for Anything—was a motto engrained in him since childhood. Both his parents had served in the army and taught him the values of service and hard work. He'd followed their example and selected West Point for college then served eight years in the army. Joining the FBI had become his objective after witnessing a murder on base. It haunted him that he hadn't been able to stop that death. So now his job was to remove killers from society and thereby save lives.

He stood and proceeded into the police station, straight to the chief's office. "Chief, I believe Detective Reid could be in danger. I found her phone on the ground outside with a broken screen. Both she and her car are gone. I was waiting for her to drive past so I could follow her to the crime scene. One of your officers saw her car head east."

Chief Gunther's face paled. "Let's not rush to conclusions. She may have dropped her phone getting into her car and gotten a lead she needed to check out in a hurry. Do you have her phone?"

"I didn't touch it in case it's evidence." The image of Charlotte as a prisoner of a psychotic murderer would not leave his head. "Had she received any threats lately? Any other cases she was working that would cause someone to hold a grudge and want to hurt her?"

"No recent case comes to mind." The chief scratched his chin. "I'll put out a notice over the police radio and have officers search the parking lot."

The action plan did little to ease Austin's worry. "The video footage from the surveillance camera outside will show what happened. Can you access that?"

"Will take a minute but I can." The chief put on his reading glasses and clicked around on the computer. After a minute, he picked up the phone. "My office…now," he said in a raised voice. "I need access to the video from the station's outdoor cameras. Detective Reid is missing."

Within seconds, a young man dressed in a navy polo shirt and khaki pants arrived holding a laptop. He set it on the round table in the chief's office and opened the recent video surveillance footage of the rear parking lot. "I'll fast forward until we get to the time Detective Reid left the building."

Austin watched the fast-moving images until the video slowed. First, a black car pulled into the parking lot, then moved past the sight line of the camera. Fifteen minutes

later, Charlotte appeared. She walked off toward the rear
of the lot before disappearing from view. A few minutes
later, her car drove toward the exit and out of sight. The
tech played that last section again. Though the image wasn't
clear, the driver of the car didn't look like Charlotte.

"The black car is still there, parked in the back corner
where I found Charlotte's phone. We need Forensics to
go through it." Austin rubbed his forehead, fighting the
headache squeezing his temples. A small-town department
didn't have a large team of crime scene techs. They relied
mostly on the parish or state resources. And those they did
have were likely busy on the murder investigation.

"I'll request a crime scene team from Kingston Parish,"
the chief said. "What kind of person kidnaps an officer in
broad daylight?"

"Someone brazen and confident. This person is either
taunting the police or eager enough to cause harm. Or both."
Austin grew nauseous. One person fit the profile. A serial
killer who got bolder each time he killed without being
caught.

When arriving in Presque, Austin had been anxious
about seeing Charlotte again. They'd ended their previous
working partnership on not great terms. The fact he'd kissed
her the week of Charlotte's sister being found murdered
had soured any potential relationship. Austin should have
kept his focus on the assignment. Instead, he'd fallen for
the detective he'd been paired with. His professional integrity, which he held to the highest standard, had slipped. He
hadn't solved the case and left town with a stinging heart.
Getting emotionally involved in a case always ended badly.

Before meeting Charlotte six years ago, he'd ruled out
romance and marriage. Witnessing multiple failed marriages of his coworkers at the Bureau had made him deter-

mined to stay far away from a committed relationship. The job was demanding and emotionally brutal. Agents carried guilt, grief and anger as often as they carried a badge and service weapon.

But for a brief time, Charlotte had begun to alter his beliefs. He'd opened himself to the possibility of love but then reality had slammed the door closed. Charlotte had blamed both Austin and herself for not catching the killer in time to save her sister. Remorse had driven a wedge between them.

He studied the computer screen. Nothing mattered more than finding Charlotte—safe and alive.

"I'll review it again in slow motion and see if I can spot anything we missed," the tech said.

"I can't wait." The perpetrator's awareness of the police department surveillance cameras didn't surprise Austin. He'd studied the Presque Killer going all the way back to the start of the man's criminal life in Baton Rouge. In the beginning, the perpetrator kidnapped and strangled but did not kill his victims, who had shown the same ligature strangle marks on their necks. When the thrill of kidnapping and torture faded, the killer had escalated his choices. Kidnap in Baton Rouge and dump the body in Presque. Finally, he killed in Presque, where he earned notoriety and his nickname.

Since Ruby's murder six years ago, the last known one until yesterday, Austin had studied this killer. A profile had been compiled by the FBI Behavior Science Unit. Austin had assumed he could read the killer's thoughts and intentions. Many serial killers, like the Presque Killer, snatched young women who had at-risk lifestyles. People who wouldn't be reported missing for a time or not at all. This killer liked the feeling of control and overpowering the weak. But the fact that he'd abducted a detective as physically fit as Charlotte, though, had Austin tossing all his theories out the window. Perhaps taking Charlotte was the start of a chess match the killer assumed he'd win. Austin needed to clear his mind of what he thought he knew and simply assess the facts before him.

"I'm heading out to search. Call me if you learn anything." He left the office, moving with speed to the front of the station and to his SUV. Where to start? Six years had passed since the last cluster of murders. Those murders had been spaced months apart. Had the killer resumed with an intensified instinct for murder? Or had he been active all this time in another part of the country? Murders that fit this killer's profile would have gotten Austin's attention, though.

Austin peeled away from the curb and headed in the direction the officer had earlier indicated. His gaze scanned the streets for any sign of Charlotte's car. Thirty minutes had passed since she'd been driven away. Chief Gunther mentioned that his police force didn't have the resources for GPS trackers on their vehicles. His hands tightened on the steering wheel. She could be so far out of town that they might never find her.

The first thing Charlotte noticed was the smell, reminiscent of a musty basement. A lethargic fog remained inside her brain. She was sleepy and fought the urge to descend back into the blackness. Snippets of her memory returned like looking through a stack of photographs. She'd been inside her car. Her current case and Ruby on her mind. A poke to her neck. The voice of a man behind her. A hidden face. A threat that terrified her.

The reality of her situation slapped her into an alert state.

She'd been kidnapped by the Presque Killer. Had Ruby held the same terror Charlotte was feeling?

Her vision was obscured by a piece of fabric tied around her head, covering her eyes. The fabric brushed against her lashes as she blinked. Charlotte glanced down to take in a sliver of low light that the blindfold allowed in. She made out a small portion of her lap. Tugging on her hands, she couldn't free them from the binds that tied behind her. She was seated in a hard chair. The sound of a vehicle engine coming from outside grew louder then quieted. If she could free herself from the ties, she could escape before her captor reappeared.

She made small kicks with her feet, rubbing the soles of her shoes across a smooth floor. Her ankles were bound as well. Charlotte worked both her feet and hands to loosen the cords. After a few minutes, she regained her full awareness and her efforts increased. The cord around her ankles had loosened but not enough for her to move freely. The binds around her wrists remained tight, cutting into her skin. Her fingers tingled and started to go numb.

A door banged closed somewhere above, then footsteps thumped on nearby stairs. She stilled and dropped her chin. If he thought she was still knocked out, maybe he'd leave again. Charlotte slowed her breathing yet kept her body tense for a quick reaction in case of attack.

"You're much prettier than your sister." The man's voice held the same digital quality as in the car. He must be using something to alter his voice. "Then again, you're not a junkie. I did you a favor, really. Isn't it a relief not to constantly worry about your troubled little sis?"

He'd connected Charlotte with Ruby, one of his victims. Ice shards of pain dug into Charlotte's skin. She didn't react.

She had to keep calm and in control and not allow the killer to rattle her nerves.

"I only want to talk," he continued. "Then I'll let you go. It's not your death I'm after. At least not yet." He chuckled. "You get an advantage I've never given anyone else. You will know the rules of the game."

A game? Was that what he considered murder? "I'm not interested," she mumbled through the gag tied over her mouth. She'd engage him with caution. If he did let her go, she'd have information to use in the hunt to capture him.

"You don't have a choice." The sound of his footsteps grew closer. "I'm the game master. I make the rules. You get the opportunity to play."

An opportunity to play for what? The question burned her throat. For her life? She tilted her head in an attempt to glimpse the person taunting her, but the room was too dark to see much past her feet.

"You get the chance to be the hero, Charlotte. You get another chance to try and catch me." He let out a raspy laugh. "Not that you ever will."

His hot breath brushed the side of her face, and she recoiled.

"Listen closely." He coughed, then cleared his throat. "The game begins the moment I release you. The rules are simple. Starting today, I will take prisoners. Women I find pleasing to the eye. I haven't decided how many I'll take yet. Like fishing, I may get lucky one day and strike out the next. If you find and stop me in seven days, you win. The women go free and they can return to their miserable normal lives." The man's fingers loosened the knot of the gag covering her mouth.

When it fell, she sucked in air. "And if I don't?" Her heart pounded.

The man chuckled. "When the clock strikes midnight on next Thursday, seven days and twelve hours from now, they all die. And I come for you. Your life, Charlotte Reid, will be my reward for a job well done."

Her blood ran cold. "I'll catch you before this day is done. You'll spend the rest of your life locked in a jail cell."

"Promises, promises." His voice sounded from behind her. "This was why I wanted you to play. You couldn't save your sister. How does that make you feel, Charlotte, that you didn't keep her safe?"

She tensed, anticipating another injection or a blow to the head. "You'll pay for what you did to Ruby and those other girls." Since she was young, Charlotte had felt a responsibility to protect her little sister. During their years in foster care and school, Charlotte had stood up to every bully. She'd been there to pick up the broken pieces each time Ruby shattered. They'd had a rough childhood, abandoned by their mother and sent into the system. Charlotte had managed to survive with a few emotional bruises, mostly due to her guarded heart. She'd sought a career in law enforcement to help her community. Ruby, on the other hand, the more sensitive one, had been buried under the pressure of trauma.

"Did you murder the poor girl we found last night in the ditch?" Would pride in his crime elicit a confession?

"That's for you to figure out, Detective. Didn't you used to love puzzles? You won't put together the one I made for you in time."

Fury had Charlotte attempting to rise off the chair. With her feet bound and her arms tied behind her, she stumbled and almost fell forward. A combination of willpower and pure rage kept her balanced. She lowered the legs of the chair down to the floor. "Let me go and get on with it. Unless deep down you're afraid of what I will do to you."

His laughter didn't convey humor. Cruelty tinted the edges. "Your confidence is impressive. Remember, if you fail, people will die, including yourself." He relieved some of the tension in the cord around her wrist. "With a little effort, you should be able to work loose the ties and free your feet. You're in a basement in a house outside of town. I disabled your car. A long walk will get you back to the police station. I have no ties to this house and I won't return. You can have your techs comb the place for DNA evidence but you won't find any. You're good at your job. I'm better."

"We'll see about that," she ground out through clenched teeth. Charlotte went to work freeing her hands. The sound of footsteps fading as her captor went upstairs spurred her on. The cord fell onto the ground at the same moment a car engine roared to life. Had he parked a getaway vehicle ahead of time? *Hurry.* She untied the binding around her ankles and lowered the blindfold, stopping for a second to notice the color of the cord—red. The same type and color the Presque Killer used to bind and strangle.

His sick game pushed her off-balance. Kidnap women and if he was not stopped in seven days, the women would die. And so would Charlotte. Why had he selected her? Was he exploiting the sore spot in her heart from the murder of her sister and her past failure to catch him? He'd mentioned her love of puzzles, something she'd enjoyed as a child. She'd found fitting together hundreds of little pieces to be a way to gain control of her chaotic life.

She swallowed hard and took stock of her surroundings. The stairs and door to the basement room lay directly ahead. She charged through and up the stairs, ignoring the pins and needles tingling in her arms and legs. On the first floor, she halted in the kitchen. Everything appeared like the family living here had cleaned up before heading out of town. Perhaps they were on vacation and the killer had taken advantage of an empty house. Charlotte tried the landline phone and heard no dial tone. Either someone had tampered with the line or the homeowners had disconnected it in preference of cell phones.

She went outside and over by the driveway, which stretched about a quarter mile to the road. Nothing about this house or area seemed familiar. No neighbors were visible because of the trees surrounding the property.

Her car had been parked by the garage door. She went inside the car and searched for her keys and phone. The keys were in the cup holder. Her phone was nowhere to be found—probably tossed somewhere so it couldn't be traced to her location. She turned the key but the engine wouldn't turn over. True to his word, her kidnapper had disabled her car. The folder with her crime scene information had been moved to the back seat. Had the killer enjoyed reviewing the results of his labor? She grabbed the folder and tucked it under her arm.

Guess she was walking back to town. If she was lucky, she'd flag down a passing motorist for help.

Before leaving, she mentally noted the exterior of the house. When she got to the end of the driveway, she'd find the address listed on the mailbox.

Though her muscles trembled, her resolve firmed with every step. Charlotte didn't care about being a hero. No award would be as satisfying as seeing her sister's killer convicted of murder and sentenced to a life behind bars. God punished the wicked, and she offered her assistance to make sure the punishment fit the crimes. If the Presque Killer wanted a game, she'd play. She would win.

THREE

Austin's cell phone rang. He pulled off on the side of the road and answered the call without looking at the caller ID. "Agent Walsh."

"It's Chief Gunther. Detective Reid has been recovered. A citizen found her walking on a road about five miles outside of the town limits. She's on her way to the station and should be here in ten minutes."

Austin exhaled a long breath. Relief flooded through him. But new worries popped into his head. "Is she hurt? Does she need medical attention?"

"She's spitting mad but otherwise fine. She said that the man who took her let her go. I requested a Kingston Parish forensics team go through the house and her car. The abductor's black car as well. The one left here at the station. It appears to be stolen."

Could it be the person who'd kidnapped Charlotte wasn't the Presque Killer? A serial killer, as a general practice, did not regress in their tactics.

Austin ended the call, then returned to the station. He waited outside in the parking lot, in the heat, for Charlotte to arrive. When she exited the car of another officer, Austin couldn't suppress his smile. She did look mightily perturbed, but clearly ready to push her way through all the concerned officers waiting for her to get to her desk and back to work.

He stood against the brick building, taking advantage of the small amount of shade it offered, and studied her. The tragedy of her sister's death had hardened her, and he desired to smooth over those sharp edges of her facial features.

While accepting a pat on the back from a male officer, she glanced in his direction. Their gazes connected.

For a moment, the world stood still. He blinked, and events continued spinning. If he couldn't remain emotionally unattached from the case and the lead detective, he'd complicate their work. And complications on an already difficult investigation wouldn't be tolerated. Even the slightest error or missed clue meant a killer remained free.

As Charlotte walked toward him, Austin pushed off the building and into the sunlight. He took a few strides before meeting up with her. "I'm glad you're okay." *Keep it professional.* He sealed away the panic he'd felt while she was missing. "Can we talk about what happened? I need to know everything."

Her eyebrows arched. "Can I take a minute to gather my thoughts and get a drink?"

He mentally swatted himself. *You can be a professional and not be a jerk.* "Of course. I'm sorry. You've been through a lot today. Should you be checked out by a doctor first?"

"Not necessary. We made a quick stop at my doctor's office. They took blood and urine samples. They'll call if anything from the tests is concerning. Besides the shot that knocked me out, which has worn off, I wasn't harmed. Actually…he made an effort not to hurt me. My wrists have a few nylon rope burns from where he tied me but he wanted to release me in fighting shape. I will need

to give a statement and have my wrists swabbed and photographed."

He should halt their conversation. Escort her inside to
cool off, sit down and drink a tall glass of cold water. But
his need for information was too urgent. "Do you have any
idea who this guy is?"

"I didn't see him or recognize his voice but it was the
Presque Killer. The man who murdered Ruby." She gri-
maced. "He's connected me to Ruby and taunted me with
her death. This psychopath thinks this is all a game."

"What did he say he wants from you?" A weight settled in his chest. He'd studied cases with serial killers who
fashioned themselves to be ring leaders in their own cir-
cus. They cracked the whip and made everyone perform
to their tune.

"To be a player in his twisted world." Charlotte glanced
over her shoulder—her face tense. "Let's go inside and talk
somewhere private. It's bad, Walsh. What he plans to do
is really bad."

Charlotte's gaze scanned her desk, searching to make
sure she'd gathered all the files she wanted to bring along,
before she glanced up at Austin. He'd stationed himself at
the other side of her desk. His hawklike eyes watched everything going on around them.

Immediately when she'd arrived at the station, she'd sat
down with the chief and Austin. Her tale of the events that
transpired left them both at a loss for words. State police
had been notified. All regional law enforcement stood on
high alert.

She slipped a trembling hand into the front pocket of her
pants. Her earlier adrenaline had left her body, resulting
in the desire to take a long, deep nap. The abduction had

taken a toll on her, but there was no way she'd admit it. She would charge on. The Presque Killer wouldn't deter her, despite his threat to her life. She couldn't dwell on the danger.

"I still want to revisit the crime scene in the daylight. You should have a look too before more time passes." She placed the stack of remaining files she'd removed from document boxes into a desk drawer and locked it. "We can come back afterward and go over all the files from the prior cases. It's been a while since you laid eyes on them." Charlotte, on the other hand, checked out the cold case files every couple of months to keep the details fresh. She refused to allow the victims to be forgotten. In all her examinations, she hadn't found anything substantial to provide a break in the case.

"I'll drive," Austin said while raising an eyebrow. "I want to make sure you don't take off on me again."

"I see you haven't lost your grim since of humor." A smile tugged at the corners of her lips. Her department-issued car, which had been towed back to the station, was under lockdown while they waited for the crime scene techs to arrive. She doubted they'd find anything useful. Same with the house where she'd been held captive. The Presque Killer was careful. But then he had revealed he was familiar enough with her to connect her to Ruby. That felt significant. Had he tipped his hand by selecting her to participate in his sick plan?

"Let's go, then." Austin halted in the hallway leading to the outside door and faced her. "When I get in work mode, I put on blinders. The person who took you also murdered your sister. I haven't forgotten how that tragedy affected you. Trust that I've got your back."

She knew he meant professionally. Personally, she couldn't help but remember that he'd abandoned her when she needed him the most. Despite her lingering lack of faith in his commitment to the Presque cases, her cheeks warmed under his intense gaze. "I'll worry about my emotional state when I know he's locked away and can't hurt anyone else." Not the healthiest way to deal with the situation but it was the best she could manage at the moment.

Austin pushed open the door and held it while she left the building. "My vehicle is the black SUV with tinted windows."

"Did the car rental company give you the FBI special?"

A small smile crept onto his face. The only way to stay sane during times like this was to allow humor to surface occasionally.

While he walked around the hood to get to the passenger side, she looked him over. Same dark hair with the same crisp haircut. Still smooth-shaven, showing off a dimple in the center of his chin. Austin was tall and athletically built—with more of a soccer player physique than football linebacker. He was classically handsome and carried the serious air that came with the weight of his job. He seemed more intense now than the last time they'd worked together, with his posture more erect and confident. A combination most women couldn't resist. She noticed the absence of a wedding ring on his left hand when he got into the SUV. Why was he still single?

"The Bureau rents cars for agents on field assignments, so I guess I do get the cliché special-agent-mobile." He slipped on a pair of aviator sunglasses. "Lead the way."

She provided directions as he drove to the crime scene.

Good thing her self-control had been reinforced with titanium bars. Austin signified a time in her life she could never return to. A moment when she'd forgotten her mission and let down her guard. Ruby had paid the price for her distraction. Charlotte vowed to never allow her feelings to take her focus away from her job. Not anger, fear, or frustration—or falling in love.

As he drove, Austin replayed Charlotte's account of her kidnapping and the killer's evil plan. The Presque Killer wanted more than a kill. He desired attention and to prove he could outsmart them all. Why involve Charlotte? Because she was the lead detective who'd been hunting him for years. Or was it for a more personal reason?

Austin pulled over to the side of the road where yellow crime scene tape marked off a large square. When he exited the car, his nose filled with the scents of fish and a faint sulfur produced from rotting vegetation. The scene would be released soon. With no breeze, the tape sagged, looking forlorn. The isolated area probably saw minimal traffic. "Were there any tire tracks of interest?"

"It hasn't rained much lately, so the dry gravel road didn't offer much. No footprints either. It appears the killer cleaned up where he'd stepped." She wiped something away from the corner of her eye. "Like before, the killer left little behind other than the body."

Mucky swamp bordered both sides, and appeared to go back at least a hundred feet from the road. The vegetation wasn't too thick, which was why the body had been spotted not long after it had been dumped.

Charlotte removed three large, glossy photographs from a protective sleeve. She handed him one of the photos. "Here's a wide view of what was found."

No matter how many years he did this job, the sight of a defiled corpse sickened him. He took his sensitivity as a good sign. The day he felt nothing at a crime scene was the day he left the FBI. "Was anything discovered in the area that tied back to the victim or possibly the killer?"

"Her purse was found hanging on the branch of that tree." She indicated where. "No ID was inside. Only a small amount of cash."

He studied the photograph, then stepped closer to the area the victim had been placed. "This woman was posed in a similar manner to the prior victims. From what I recall, that information wasn't released to the public."

"No, it wasn't. Our victim matches the profile of the others… Caucasian, younger female in her twenties. They all had blond hair with the exception of Ruby. Propofol was used to sedated the other victims, and he likely used the same medication on the recent victim and myself." Shaking her head, she crouched and gazed at the matted grass.

"Do you have a close-up of her hands?" He noticed faint lines in the dirt where the victim's fingers would have been. They might have dragged in the ground when the body was placed. Austin took out his cell phone, zooming into the area on the ground, and took pictures at different angles.

"Here." She handed him another photo. "It's not a close-up but you get a good view of her hands. What are you thinking?"

He drew on the facts he knew about the cold cases. "Strangling someone is up close and personal. We didn't find anything under the prior victims' nails. I still believe the women fought back and the killer made sure anything that might identify him was wiped clean. I've assumed he cleansed trace evidence prior to moving the bodies."

"I know my sister did." Charlotte put on a pair of black-rimmed glasses and lowered to a crouch. "The killer taunted me with his knowledge of my love of puzzles as a child. I've a hard time believing I have a connection to the killer."

Austin considered the possibility. "He knows you, whether through researching you during your investigation or having some sort of a prior relationship with you. When we get back to the station, let's make a list of men you know who may fit the profile. See if any correspond to our suspect list from the older cases. Who knows, we may get a match."

She removed a pair of latex gloves from her pants pocket and slipped them on. Her fingers combed through the blades of grass as her eyes searched for anything left behind. "My sister and I spent time in foster care after my mom went to jail. She died prior to her release, so we aged out of the system. We came across a lot of people during those years, from the families who cared for us to fellow foster kids. It may be a stretch. We don't have time to chase dead ends."

"In this type of investigation we chase every lead." He lowered himself and searched the ground along with her. "Your history in foster care may not be connected but you considered the possibility, therefore it's worth digging into."

"Look, red fibers." She used a tweezer to lift up several. "They found more imbedded in her neck."

He opened the evidence bag he'd been keeping in his hand. After the fibers were inside, he sealed the bag. "I'll put in a request to contact the stores in the area. Let's find out if anyone's recently sold the brand of red cord we identified during our last investigation."

She stood, set her hands on her hips and sighed. "I wonder if the killer has been hiding in plain sight under my nose the entire time. Do serial killers take breaks before starting up again?"

"The human psyche is complicated." Austin swatted away the swarm of mosquitoes that had descended on him. "It's not often that a ritualistic killer stops cold turkey. He could have experienced a change in his life that made engaging in his prior activities more difficult. There's the possibility he moved and killed elsewhere but I believe his pattern would have been picked up by the FBI's CODIS database. In cases where a killer pauses, something triggers him to resume. An event occurs that reignites his urges."

"Whatever happened, it must have been big. Our killer hasn't returned simply to murder. He's issued a challenge with deadly consequences."

A threat to innocent women, including Charlotte. Another strong motivation to catch the killer. "I won't leave this time until our job is done. When I board a plane for home, the man who kidnapped you will be securely behind bars."

FOUR

Raindrops splattered on the windshield of Austin's SUV as they drove south to Baton Rouge. Charlotte stared out the window, wondering how a place so full of beauty and life could sustain such dark evil. She'd grown up in various towns in the area, including Presque, first with her mom and then through the foster care system. As an adult, Charlotte had found a home and a career in Presque. If only Ruby had felt the same. Instead of reaching for success, Ruby couldn't stay clean long enough to hold employment for more than a few months. For Charlotte, the most tragic piece of Ruby's murder was that Ruby had been clean and sober for almost two months leading up to her death. Her postmortem toxicology reports had indicated no drugs were found in her system. Ruby had been at the starting point of a new life, which had been stolen from her. But now there was a chance the killer had been connected to Charlotte. Had Charlotte somehow been the reason that a new life had been taken away from Ruby?

Austin parked in the lot of the medical examiner's office in Baton Rouge. The body of last night's victim had been brought here for assessment. Instead of speaking to the ME over the phone, they'd agreed viewing the body in person would provide more benefits to their investigation.

"How are you holding up?" Austin's brow furrowed with concern.

He's probably questioning whether I can emotionally handle working this investigation. She took in a deep breath. "These visits are never easy, but I'll be okay. I can't let my feelings cloud my vision." Her mind flashed back to six years ago, when she'd stepped into the same building on separate occasions to view the bodies of the initial four victims. After seeing her sister laying lifeless on a cold metal table, draped with a sheet, Charlotte had run outside to throw up in the hedges alongside the building.

"Let me know if you need a break or to step outside and get some air. I'll do the same." He exited the car and opened the door to the back seat to collect his messenger bag.

While he might be doubting her fortitude, Austin also was being considerate. He'd shown the same concern the last time they'd worked together. Her anger had blocked out the good she'd witnessed in his character. He'd often checked in on her emotional and physical state, even more so after Ruby's death. Until he left and all his care and concern no longer mattered. If Austin had really wanted to protect her, he would have attempted to stay.

She entered the building and introduced herself to the woman at the front desk.

Soon, an assistant greeted the two of them in the lobby, then waved them forward and down the hall. "Protective gear is located in the lockers by the doors to the room but I'm sure you already know that. This isn't your first trip to the medical examiner's office." He guided them to the area. "I need to collect the body and bring her into the room. Holler if you need anything." He hustled away to his next task.

"He's the friendliest person I've ever met at the ME's office." In her prior experience, the employees who worked here were somber and academic—expected traits for those whose job was to study the dead.

Charlotte and Austin dressed in protective gowns, gloves, booties and hats.

When she stepped inside, she sucked in a breath at the cold air. Despite being prepared for the change in temperature, it took her a few minutes to fight off the chill. Viewing the body of a murder victim always left her feeling like she'd never be warm again.

The medical examiner appeared through a door in the rear of the room, fully garbed in protective garments. He wasn't wearing eye protection or a face shield as they wouldn't be required for viewing the body. "Welcome." Dr. Connor held out a gloved hand to both Charlotte and Austin. "I've completed the initial examination. We're still waiting for some of the results of the lab tests." He flipped over the metal cover of a clipboard and scanned several pages. "The female victim was found to have opioids in her system at the time of death. She had some food in her stomach. Time of death is determined to be sixteen hours prior to the discovery of her body."

The rear door opened again and the same assistant who'd brought them back now wheeled a table inside. On the table lay the body of a female. Blond hair framed her lifeless face. Most of her body was covered with a white sheet. The assistant brought the table into the center of the room and locked the wheels, leaving it underneath a set of large lights secured to the ceiling.

"Thank you, Robert," Dr. Connor said to his assistant. "Alert the lab that the tissue samples we just collected are ready to be processed. Make sure they know I need those results back as soon as possible."

"I'm on it," Robert replied. "Anything else you need from me right now?"

"Nothing in here." Dr. Connor turned his attention to the body on the table, after which his assistant exited the room.

Charlotte gazed down at the pale face of the murdered woman. "Have you determined an official cause of death?"

"Strangulation," Dr. Connor stated. "The opioids in her system may have hastened her death. But there's no doubt the ligature marks on her neck indicate a rope or cord was used to cut off her air supply." He pointed to the markings that circled her neck.

"I was told she had a crescent moon carved in her arm." Charlotte's eyes stung with tears she fought to hold back. She had to clear her mind of everything besides the data being presented.

Dr. Connor lifted the top of the sheet, exposing the woman's arm, creamy white except for a red mark.

At the sight of the design, an exact match to the one left on Ruby and the other victims, bile rose in Charlotte's throat.

"There are too many similarities to our group of victims six years ago." Austin leaned in to get a closer look at the symbol marked on the woman's arm. "We have to be dealing with the same killer." He moved his gaze down the woman's arm to her hands. "Did you swab under her fingernails?"

"I swabbed both under her nails and around each fingertip for evidence." Dr. Connor checked his paperwork, then logged into the nearby computer. "Those tests haven't been completed yet. I didn't see much from a visual inspection but most trace evidence isn't visible, even under a magnifying glass."

"Were her nails dirty?" Austin straightened, then glanced down at the victim's hands once again. "I noticed markings in the ground at the crime scene that may have been made by her fingertips dragging when her body was placed."

After a few clicks of the mouse, Dr. Connor pulled up

color photographs taken during the examination and autopsy. "The fingers and nails look clean." He zoomed in to focus on the victim's left hand.

Charlotte studied the image. "Perhaps the markings you saw at the crime scene were from something else." The victim's nails appeared clean to Charlotte as well. Were they too clean? Surely the killer wouldn't have taken the time to scrub the body at the dump site.

"Perhaps." Austin had removed a notepad from his bag and was writing rapidly.

"Anything else of note?" Charlotte asked. The room had begun to feel tight, like the walls were closing in at small increments. The air tasted bitter and stung her lungs. As strongly as the urge struck her to race out the door, she held her feet firmly in place. This was not the time to run.

Austin listened closely to Dr. Connor's verbal autopsy report and jotted down significant information in his personal notebook. He'd receive the final report from the ME within the next few days, dependent on the return of test results. His hope that they'd found trace evidence, such as the killer's DNA underneath her nails, sank at the sight of her overly clean hands. The Presque Killer had only left one small DNA sample on the first victim, which hadn't matched to anyone in the system. A second sample might not bring them closer to identifying the killer but would tie together this new murder with the older ones. However, there was no doubt in anyone's mind that the same individual had killed and dumped all five women.

Austin and Charlotte's phones pinged with an incoming email. Charlotte had picked up a replacement phone on their way to Baton Rouge.

"They identified the victim," Austin said, reading the

email. "Ginny Gerard. Twenty-two-year-old female. Last known address in Watson, Louisiana."

"That's not far from here." Charlotte's gaze was fixed on her phone screen, taking in the information provided in the email. "About half way between Baton Rouge and Presque."

"Ginny Gerard was last seen at a nightclub in Baton Rouge three days ago." No surprise that the killer hunted in more populated areas, where his actions could go unnoticed. All five victims had been dumped in the area around Presque. Austin believed the killer was a local to Presque or someone who knew the community. Small towns had many observant eyes and chatty mouths. He doubted an outsider could have conducted his activity unnoticed.

"I'll call the Baton Rouge Police Department and request a detective canvas the area where Ms. Gerard was last known to be," Charlotte said. "A local cop will be better acquainted with the neighborhood and the people there."

"A city cop also may make the locals unwilling to talk." He'd witnessed the scene play out too many times. Residents grew suspicious of their police department. Fear led to sealed lips. If people had information, they refused to share it with anyone else but one another.

Charlotte nodded in agreement to Austin's concern. "Let's give them a chance and see what they come up with. First thing tomorrow morning, I want to get out the old case files and review everything."

He checked the time. How was it already seven o'clock? He hadn't eaten lunch or dinner. Then again, homicide damped a person's appetite. "Thank you for your time and the information." Austin shook Dr. Connor's hand. "Please send us your final report as soon as it's available."

"Absolutely." The medical examiner gazed at Charlotte. "How are you holding up? Reliving this can't be easy."

Dr. Connor had performed the autopsies on all the Presque Killer victims. He must remember Charlotte's struggle to view her sister's corpse in this same room. Austin would never forget that horrible day. He'd felt helpless watching Charlotte trying hard not to shatter.

"I won't lie and say it's easy coming here. If we had caught the murderer six years ago, this young woman wouldn't have ended up on your exam table." She quickly wiped the corner of her eye.

"He will be held accountable." Austin placed a protective hand low on Charlotte's back and guided her out of the room. This time, the Presque Killer had given an ultimatum. The investigation had been given a deadline. If they failed, Charlotte would pay with her life. An electric charge ran through Austin. He would not fail.

On the return trip to Presque, he listened to Charlotte's phone conversations with the Baton Rouge PD and Chief Gunther. Her professionalism and efficient work style continued to impress him. Nothing about Charlotte was ordinary. Her blonde hair, styled in its usual ponytail, reminded him of a ray of sunshine. She was fit and strong yet gentle when handling the families of victims. Her knowledge made her a good detective. Her empathy made her an extraordinary law enforcement officer.

Austin had struggled with the personal aspect of his job since joining the FBI. He loved reading and learning, which he found easy enough. What proved difficult was keeping in mind the fact that real people were affected by the crimes he studied. But working with Charlotte had provided him with lessons he hadn't learned at the training academy. How to talk to a witness without getting their guard up. What to say during conversations with victims' families and what not to share. When Austin had returned to his home office, he'd carried Charlotte's example going forward when working other cases. Like his last one in Oregon, during which he'd tracked and captured a killer who'd preyed on backpackers. His improved interpersonal skills helped him be a better special agent while retaining the aloofness he needed to avoid emotional burnout.

He glanced at Charlotte. Did she know how deeply he admired her?

When he parked in front of her house, a longing filled him. For what exactly, he couldn't tell. To return home at the end of the day to a family? That dream would never become a reality. His line of work demanded complete commitment. Nights, weeks, months spent traveling created fractures in even the best relationships. Marriages of fellow special agents that Austin considered strong had crumbled under the weight of a demanding profession. A woman as special as Charlotte deserved better. She was deeply rooted in this community while his job required constant travel.

She reached for the door handle, then paused. "Let's plan to meet at six tomorrow morning at the station. I'll ask for the evidence boxes to be brought up to the conference room."

"I'll bring coffee and doughnuts." He pushed back a yawn. His day had started before dawn. The travel, combined with the stress of Charlotte's kidnapping and the pressure to catch a serial killer, weighed heavy.

"I've come to accept that it was a good thing the FBI sent you back to Presque. I'd hate to have to bring up to speed a new agent." She appeared resigned. "I'm sorry for how we ended things last time. And for how I acted before you left," she added with a grin.

"I regret not pushing back on the orders to return to my home office." Although, even if he had, the likelihood of his supervisor granting his request would've been slim. Even

Caleb would have had a tough time convincing FBI leadership that Austin's time was best served in Presque. After months of few leads, little evidence and no viable suspects, he wasn't surprised when the Bureau had directed its resources elsewhere. The cases he'd worked on since he left Presque six years ago had been important too. Each case had value. He'd witnessed numerous dangerous predators taken off the streets. Every solved case hardened his determination to keep fighting for justice. He couldn't allow his tender feelings for Charlotte to cause a special attachment to the Presque cases. Still, he had to see these cases closed. The victims' families deserved justice. "I never forgot about the Presque victims." *Or you*, he almost added.

"That's reassuring." She clutched her purse on her lap. "I need a partner who wants this killer caught as much as I do."

"Charlotte, the madman threatened your life along with countless others." The thought of her under the control of a vicious killer heated his blood. "Do you feel safe sleeping at home tonight?" She'd lived alone six years ago, but the idea she might be in a relationship knocked him off-balance.

She gazed at the cottage-style house with only the front porch light providing an illuminating glow. "I have seven days to find and stop him. If he wanted to harm me sooner, he would have earlier today."

Her logic didn't settle his anxiety. "I'm staying at the Magnolia Hotel. It's not far away, so if you need anything or hear a bump in the night, call me. I'll be over in a flash."

"Good to know my FBI partner is also a superhero." Charlotte opened the SUV door and stepped outside. "The FBI couldn't find you a better place to stay than the Magnolia?" Standing beside the vehicle, she leaned over to peer in and said after a pause, "On second thought, that is the nicest hotel in Presque. They spray for cockroaches, which is the best standard of quality around these parts. See you tomorrow."

At the mention of cockroaches, he shivered. Austin considered himself brave and had faced down many bad guys with guns, but creepy-crawlies sent him running in the other direction. After Charlotte closed the door, he waited for her to get safely inside her house. Instead of driving to his hotel, he got out and did a perimeter check of her property. Blame his time in the army for his hypervigilance. These circumstances warranted extra precaution, though.

While he searched for hidden danger, memories of his time in the service drifted into his mind. Mostly good recollections. Several he'd fought over the years to banish. Witnessing the murder on base was a bad memory he didn't want to forget because it stoked the fire he needed to do his job. He'd thought he could stop the men fighting as he raced toward them on the base's recreation field. Austin hadn't gotten there in time to stop the stabbing. There was nothing he could do to prevent a fellow soldier from dying. He had helped capture the soldier who'd murdered another and in doing so, stopped future violence. Sometimes, that was all a person could do.

When he decided all was quiet and clear, he returned to his car, then took a slow drive around the block. The sun had set. The streets were relatively quiet. Most houses had a few lights on inside. He passed Charlotte's house again and saw one light on in the front room. He prayed she'd find restful sleep tonight. Austin knew sleep would elude him until the killer was taken off the streets.

FIVE

Charlotte managed to get a few hours' rest. Even before the first beams of sunlight breached her curtains, she rolled out of bed and started a pot of coffee. She had about an hour before meeting Austin at the station. With a little luck and guidance from God, they'd find a clue missed before, which would lead them to the Presque Killer's identity. He had to be stopped before he harmed anyone else.

Last night, she'd dreamed about Ruby and the sweet girl she'd once been. For so many years, they'd only had each other. The killer had not only snuffed out an innocent life but stolen Charlotte's best friend. No one would ever replace Ruby in her life. How could anyone fill the giant hole in Charlotte's heart? A hole the size of a sister whom she'd shared everything with. Every good and bad day. All the trauma of witnessing their mother arrested and then never seeing her again. Moving from foster home to foster home with only one another to cling to.

Thinking about all that the killer had stolen from her and the other victims' families filled her with rage. If her life was the cost of bringing him down, she'd pay without question. Charlotte could not live another year knowing the person responsible for five cruel deaths walked free.

She showered and dressed while mentally prepping herself for the day ahead. Her phone rang, and she assumed it was Austin checking in to make sure she'd made it safely through the night. After he'd dropped her off, Charlotte had noticed him walking around the property, searching for any danger that lay hidden in the shadows. His gesture warmed her heart and also set her on guard. What she needed from the dashing FBI agent was professional, not personal. He was here to save lives and catch a killer. Once the mission was accomplished, he'd get back on a plane and fly off to work on his next case. She, on the other hand, would resume her normal life and duties. "I can't wait for the day when my biggest challenge is catching some kid who robbed the corner convenience store."

She lifted her cell phone and noticed Presque PD on the caller ID. "Hello, this is Detective Reid."

"Reid, it's the chief. There's been a report of a kidnapping. A waitress working the late shift at the Pancake Café never came home after her shift."

Her stomach churned with dread. Some small part of her had hoped the Presque Killer had been bluffing about kidnapping women. She checked the calendar, where she'd circled next Thursday in red ink—their deadline. "Are we sure she's a missing person and didn't just go somewhere else after work?"

"Her husband called the station around three a.m. in a panic," Chief Gunther said. "The missing waitress, Karen Tremont, called him at midnight when she was getting ready to leave the café. Everyone is on edge due to the Presque Killer's return. A patrol officer went to the café, which is open twenty-four hours. He spoke with the staff there and was told Mrs. Tremont left around midnight, but her car is still parked in the lot. There's no sign of her in the building or surrounding area."

While the chief was talking, Charlotte slipped on her shoes and tied the laces. "I'm on my way."

"Notify Agent Walsh and have him meet you over there. If the waitress is the first kidnapping victim of the Presque Killer, we'll need to move fast."

"Agreed." She ended the call, heart racing. Even though she preferred not to work on assumptions, the Presque Killer would be the main suspect until Charlotte had facts that proved otherwise.

She made a quick call to Austin, filling him in on the few details known so far. After locking the door behind her, she raced to her car and headed to the Pancake Café.

When she arrived, Austin came out of the building to meet her. Two Presque Police Department squad cars were parked in the gravel-covered lot, both flanking a maroon minivan with Louisiana license plates.

"Is this the waitress's van?" She moved closer and used a flashlight to peer in the side windows. The van was confirmed to belong to the waitress. Beside a littering of children's toys and some trash, the van was empty. Glancing at the squad cars, she thought back to her own kidnapping yesterday. "Move your vehicles," she commanded the nearby patrol officers. "The kidnapper could have parked on the side of the van and snatched the victim as she approached to leave."

"How do we know this woman didn't leave with someone else?" one of the patrol officers, a young man who'd barely reached the drinking age, asked.

"Go interview the employees who were working with Karen Tremont before she left and find out." She pointed a finger in the direction of the café. "Let me know if anyone has knowledge of her whereabouts. But first, move your car."

She shook her head and prayed for calm. Normally, she didn't take out her frustration on other officers. This was not a normal situation.

Once the patrol cars were moved and their tire tracks marked, Austin studied the gravel ground. He turned to examine the building about twenty feet away. "No cameras."

"I asked," Officer Evans, the older of the officers, replied. He'd been on the force for eight years with his sights set on leadership. Charlotte respected his integrity and work ethic. "No video of the inside or outside of the building. Do you want me to tape off this area?"

"Yes." Charlotte said. "This is a potential crime scene."

Officer Kagan hurried out of the café, his fresh face alive with eagerness. "One of the cooks who worked overnight took a smoke break around eleven forty-five and noticed a box truck parked next to the waitress's van. It was over there." He indicated the parking spot next to the driver's side.

"Didn't anyone find it strange Karen Tremont's van didn't leave when she left after her shift ended?" Austin's intense gaze caused Officer Kagan to move back a few steps.

"I'll go ask the cook but he didn't mention it." Officer Kagan hustled back inside.

"A box truck." Charlotte examined the ground in the space beside the van. She saw two sets of tracks. One had been established as coming from the police car. The slightly larger set caught her interest. "We need to make molds of these tracks. It's a long shot and will take more time than we have but maybe we can match the make and model of tires to a specific vehicle."

"There's a lot of box trucks driving around," Austin said as a white box truck with the decal of a delivery company on the side rumbled by. "But…we'd be negligent not to work the lead."

She took out a pair of gloves and wore one on each hand. Starting her search with the van's exterior, she stepped with awareness. Several rusty dents dotted the body of the van. Some scratches on the back appeared like marks from a key. She studied the driver's-side door, particularly the door handle. Using her own kidnapping as a reference, she imagined the killer had entered Karen's car prior to her getting in. Every surface would be dusted for prints, although experience had taught the Presque Killer was too careful not to use gloves.

The corner of something white pressed against the windshield caught her attention. She looked closer and found a small note card secured under a windshield wiper. Had he left another calling card? "Austin, I found something."

Using her gloved hands, she removed the note, deep down hoping it was an innocent advertising flyer.

One

She recognized the handwriting, each letter formed with a linear style. It was similar to the note left by the murdered body of Ginny Gerard two days ago. No doubt remained in her mind—the Presque Killer's game had begun.

Charlotte made a call to the chief, requesting the crime scene processing team arrive as quickly as possible. She'd request Chief Gunther shake a few branches to bring in more resources. Lives were on the line.

Austin accepted a paper cup from Charlotte. "Thank you. I don't know how anyone can function without a cup of coffee in the morning." He removed the plastic lid, took a cautious sip and sighed, enjoying the rich flavor at the perfect temperature. The chill of the early morning had burned away with the rising sun. In the bright daylight, the café's parking lot appeared harmless. But not long ago a woman had been surprised on her way to her vehicle after a long shift, snatched before reaching the safety of the interior. Austin shuddered to imagine how terrified she must have been to encounter a killer.

No one who'd been in the restaurant at midnight had noticed any suspicious activity. From the interviews they'd conducted so far, they'd learned Mrs. Tremont left after serving her last table, one full of high school kids. She'd been tired but smiling when she'd walked out the door.

"The killer may have dined in the café. He could have used the opportunity to stalk his victim. I want to review all the sales tickets from ten o'clock until midnight. Another waitress could have noticed a man dining alone." He drew on his knowledge of criminals. A deep well he sometimes wished he could lock away and never peer into again. Witnessing a murder while in the army had left him feeling helpless. His training at the FBI Academy at Quantico and working under Caleb had solidified his mission to hunt the predators who hunted the innocent. Cutting off the wicked from harming others was his life's goal.

A while ago, Austin had confided in Caleb about his growing frustrations at his inability to stop evil from happening in the world. Leaving behind the murder cases in Presque had almost broken his will to continue in the FBI. Shortly after he returned, Caleb had sat him down and they'd spent time in prayer together. They studied God's messages in the Bible about good and evil, justice and mercy. Austin had come to accept that many events that took place were out of his control. He couldn't protect everyone. Serving God meant fulfilling His purpose to the best of his ability. But only God was perfect, and ultimately He was in control.

"I don't believe he would risk being seen inside," Charlotte said before taking a drink of coffee. "Using my kidnapping as a model, the perp stealthily moves in, grabs his victim and gets out quick."

A Presque Police Department truck pulled into the parking lot and stopped next to the building. Chief Gunther exited, placed his Stetson on his silver-haired head, then came over to where Austin and Charlotte stood. "Do you have any leads?"

"No, sir." Charlotte stepped toward the area surrounded by crime scene tape. "Nothing was found in the van, at least nothing visible to the naked eye. We have no witnesses or anyone who noticed anything off last night. No one even noticed her van was still here until her husband called looking for her."

The chief scratched his chin. "What about the tire tracks? Do you believe the techs can cast a good enough mold to get a match on the type of tire?"

"They'll get a good cast but matching it to a specific tire and to a make and model of truck takes time." Austin's chest tightened as he counted down the days—six. An investigation this scale could take weeks if not longer. As a rule, missing person investigations had to move fast. The first forty-eight hours were critical. Unfortunately, many adults weren't reported missing for at least twenty-four hours after they were last seen, sometimes longer if they disappeared for days at a time.

"I'm setting up a task force." The command in Chief Gunther's voice couldn't be missed. "Detective Reid and Special Agent Walsh, you'll both lead the team. You're dealing with both a murder and kidnapping from a known serial killer. And the clock is ticking."

"Extra assistance is much appreciated," Charlotte said. "Have the task force members been notified?"

Austin's attention continued to be drawn by Charlotte and her fierce devotion to her work. He'd partnered with many other law enforcement professionals, but Charlotte felt like a true collaborator. What if he convinced her to join the FBI? He envisioned working alongside her on cases all over the country.

"Yes," Chief Gunther answered. "All members are meeting at the station at two this afternoon. I've tapped officers from state and parish departments. You'll have the best, but don't forget, you two are in charge. I don't trust anyone else to see this to the end."

Austin nodded. His job was easier with the full trust and empowerment of local law enforcement leadership. "I'd like to interview Mrs. Tremont's husband and friends to find out if there was anyone she could have gone with last night instead of going home. We need to make sure she's not somewhere unharmed."

"I'll let you get back to work." The chief patted Charlotte on the shoulder. "Say the word and I'll get you placed in protective custody. While I believe you to be the best detective ever to serve under my command, your safety is my priority. I couldn't live with myself if something happened to you."

Chief Gunther's statement mirrored Austin's feelings. Guarding Charlotte was as important to Austin as finding the Presque Killer. In reality, they were one and the same. But only if they arrested the killer before midnight on the seventh day.

"I appreciate your concern, Chief." Charlotte crushed her empty paper coffee cup in her fist. "I will see all these cases closed, both the cold and recent. My sister died at the hands of the Presque Killer. I have to be the one who brings him to justice."

And Austin would be with her every step of the way.

* * *

Leaving the Tremont house after speaking with Karen's husband, Charlotte held little hope the woman had decided to go out with a friend or secret lover. Karen appeared to be a devoted wife and mother who worked second shift at the café so her husband could care for their young son after he came home from his office job. The family lived in a modest house with a trimmed front yard and several colorful flower beds. Mr. Tremont's emotional state hadn't been an act, or at least Charlotte didn't believe so. He genuinely seemed distraught at his wife's disappearance.

Karen wasn't the Presque Killer's typical victim, as none of the others were either married or had children. Charlotte assumed the killer wasn't being picky while selecting his mark. He wanted a woman he could easily snatch without getting caught.

Interviewing Mr. Tremont had brought her backward in time to when Ruby went missing. Initially, Charlotte had assumed her sister had gone somewhere to get drugs and get high. Only when she couldn't find Ruby in all the usual spots had she begun to worry about Ruby's life and not just her sobriety. The panic she felt after acknowledging the possible connection of Ruby's disappearance to the Presque Killer still lingered to this day. She recognized the look in Mr. Tremont's eye—a fear so deep it pushed a person into dark places.

"Thoughts?" Austin asked as they walked to their vehicles parked on the street. Somehow, the FBI agent looked as perfect as ever. Each dark hair on his head in its place. His clothes spot-free and pressed. He'd found time to shave this morning. Must have been up even earlier than Charlotte, if he'd slept at all.

For her part, Charlotte's ponytail was in the process of

falling out: frizzy blond tendrils of hair broke free like a well-orchestrated prison break. She glanced down to see a light yellow spot on the collar of her white button-down shirt. Why did she have white in her professional wardrobe when she was a magnet for everything and anything that stained clothes?

She considered Austin's question for her thoughts, and her head spun with information, not only regarding the Tremont kidnapping but the recent murder of Ginny Gerard. Police had notified Ms. Gerard's family last evening. They hadn't realized she'd been missing, since she had sometimes disappeared into the Baton Rouge party scene for weeks at a time.

"I believe the Presque Killer is true to his word. He's taken his first kidnapping victim." She removed her car keys from her pants pocket. "We need to get to the station and comb over all the old case files. I don't believe he will give us much in terms of leads but maybe there's something in the files we missed six years ago."

"Word is spreading around town." Austin unhooked his sunglasses from the front pocket of his shirt and set them on his nose. "Women around the area will be more vigilant."

"And their extra caution will make the killer more likely to make a mistake." Charlotte prayed for God's protection of everyone in the community, especially Karen Tremont. "All we need is one slipup, one witness, one clue to point us in the right direction."

"When he held you in the basement of the house, he provided you with a clue. The killer knows you, at least at some level. His current actions are personal and he's connected them to you." He stopped on the sidewalk by Charlotte's parked car. "The killer could have selected Ruby because she's your sister."

The ground underneath her feet swayed. She'd always assumed Ruby had been selected by the Presque Killer because she was an easy target. But Austin was right. With the new knowledge the killer had provided yesterday, she had to consider the possibility that Ruby had been chosen because she was Charlotte's sister. The thought made her sick to her stomach.

"I hate to admit it but you may be right." She wrapped an arm around her midsection. The increasing heat and humidity of the morning only exacerbated her queasiness. "Let's hurry back to the station. We have about four hours until the task force meeting. Perhaps we'll have some new piece of information to share after we start digging into the old cases."

The sound of a clock ticking echoed in her head. Six days. How many more lives would the Presque Killer affect before she brought him down? *Please God, no more.*

SIX

Austin set out a fresh notepad, new pen and his cell phone in a neat row on the conference room table. He had a system, which often caused good-natured teasing. Order helped him process the facts of an investigation that usually were anything but neat and orderly.

Entering the room, Charlotte ended a call. "Officers have been dispatched to talk to friends of Karen Tremont. They've been directed to call me with pertinent information. Still no credible witnesses have come forward on Mrs. Tremont's disappearance, though the tip line that's been established is lighting up. Everyone in town has a theory."

"Have you received tips on any of the cold cases after the investigations were closed?" Austin asked with apprehension. The last thing he wanted to do was remind Charlotte that his departure had led to the murder investigations being closed.

"Sure." She lifted the lid off one of the dozen or so cardboard boxes that officers had brought up from the evidence storage locker. "Small towns are hotbeds for gossip and the behavior of one or two troublemakers always gets peoples' fingers pointed their way. I'd talk to people, ask questions, get alibis. Nothing ever rose to the level of a real lead."

He took another box and removed the lid. The smell of

musty paper and years of heartbreak washed over him. With care, he took out each folder and stacked them in four piles, one for items relating to each of the four victims. Inside each folder were notes and documents not digitally filed. His laptop sat nearby. Austin logged in and pulled up his notes from their last investigation until he found the documents he wanted. "We had two main suspects six years ago, Pete Carter and Kevin DuPont. Both had weak connections to the young women, mostly due to drug sales." He read over the files they'd compiled on both men.

"May as well start there. Where are they now?" Charlotte powered up her laptop and after clicking and typing for several minutes, she moved her gaze from the computer screen. "Pete Carter is a resident of the East Baton Rouge Parish Penitentiary." She clicked and opened another webpage. "Kevin DuPont lives in Northern California. I'll place a call to the local police department to verify his whereabouts. But he was ticketed for drunk and disorderly two days ago in his home town, so I think it's safe to rule him out."

"Did you know either of them?" Although neither man had likely been in the area recently, he wanted to tie off any loose ends.

"Only on a professional level." Charlotte pushed aside her computer and pulled out files from a box, spreading the folders on the table. "I arrested both men on drug charges years ago. I don't have any personal connection to either."

He mentally crossed Pete Carter off his suspect list. Kevin DuPont would be cleared if he was located in Northern California. "While reviewing the documents and evidence related to each murder again, maybe something will point us in a new direction."

Opening the top folder on the first pile, he took out a

glossy photograph of Mary Gury, the initial murder victim, and tacked it to the board on the wall. Mary's smiling face held no knowledge of the horror that would come. He posted photographs of the other victims from the old cases, and noticed Charlotte's face pale at the sight of her sister. "Let me know if this becomes too much." He worried about her. The last time they'd investigated Ruby's murder, Charlotte's strength couldn't be denied but no one could withstand the constant reminder of a loved one's suffering.

She took a shuddering breath and removed her gaze from the photo of Ruby. "I go through several of these boxes every other month in hopes I'll find something I missed. I hate that the man who killed my sister has been living free for all these years. And now he's stealing more lives. I face the pain of looking at the evidence because not bringing Ruby's killer to justice hurts more."

Austin registered grief along with a fierce determination in Charlotte's eyes. He wanted to touch her and absorb some of her heartache. Instead, he lowered his gaze and refocused on the task at head. Taking an evidence bag out of the box marked RUBY, he noticed its light weight. The contents listed a bracelet, earrings and nose ring. He emptied the contents on the table.

Charlotte froze at the sight of the jewelry. "We had matching bracelets." She held up her arm, and a delicate gold bracelet matching the one on the table hung from her wrist. "I'd thought about requesting it back but I felt it should stay with the rest of the evidence until her killer was caught and sentenced. Our mom gave them to us and we had them resized. It's one of the only things we had from our mom when we went into foster care." She picked up the bag with her sister's bracelet inside. "See? Matching moons— Wait, crescent moons! I didn't tie the crescent moon charm on the bracelets to the mark on each victim's arm…until now. Could the charms be related to the marks on the victims' arms?"

"It's possible." He took photos of Ruby's and Charlotte's bracelets on his phone. "The crescent moon symbol appears significant. Now let's start at the beginning and see what else we can link together."

"Mary Gury was discovered on a dirt road right on the Presque city limits." Charlotte unfolded a map of the town and outlying area then marked a red X where Mary's body had been found. "DNA not belonging to the victim was found on her sweater, which is believed to be the killer's sweat. The DNA did not match anyone in the system, and I have an alert set to notify me if a match is uploaded."

He reviewed the autopsy report completed on Mary. How had her killer not left any evidence behind except for a small dot of perspiration? "Cause of death, strangulation. Red nylon rope fibers were found in the ligature marks around her neck. A shallow laceration in the shape of a U on the inside of her arm was determined to be from her killer. Looking at the mark again, it could be a primitive attempt at a crescent moon."

"Witnesses described Ms. Gury as friendly and kind but as someone who struggled with drug addiction." Charlotte picked up a cluster of papers and fingered through them. "She was last seen leaving a party alone three nights before her body was discovered. No one knew what happened to her after she left or where she planned to go afterward."

"Was there any reason to believe the people with Ms. Gury at the party were afraid to talk?" If the perpetrator was a known violent offender in the community, fear of retribution created a cone of silence.

"I don't believe so." She scanned a few more typed reports. "Mary's mother was well respected and those who were interviewed came off as motivated to help find her killer."

He nodded at her assessment. His focus turned to victim two. "Whitney Malone."

They talked through each of the four cold cases. In all the cases, nothing new jumped out. Mary Gury, Whitney Malone, Amy Casey and Ruby Reid had disappeared without a trace until their bodies were discovered. Cause of death was the same—strangulation. The instrument used—a red nylon rope. While the mark carved into Mary's arm was a U shape. Whitney, Amy and Ruby's marks looked more evolved, like a crescent moon. The recent victim's autopsy matched closely to the other known victims of the Presque Killer. He'd developed his signature. Though with the kidnapping of Karen, he was going slightly off course. Could someone have copied him, wishing for the notoriety of the Presque Killer? Possibly. Though many of the details of the killings were kept confidential. A copycat would need to have learned the killer's methods from the killer himself or been privy to classified information.

"How do we catch a ghost?" Charlotte tossed a thick file folder onto the table, then rubbed her forehead. "We've arrived at the same dead ends that stopped us before."

Dead ends that resulted in his removal from the cases and then the cases growing cold. "Do any of the victims besides Ruby have a connection to you?"

"No, other than how they looked." She wrapped her arms around her body. "I didn't put the connection together before or maybe didn't want to but all of the first three victims were white females with blond hair, like myself. Each of them was approximately my height and weight. Of course,

Ruby is my sister and we resemble each other. I don't want to believe the killer is targeting women who look like me."

The theory had come to his mind after Charlotte gave an account of her kidnapping. The killer had a strong association with Charlotte, and so far only the killer was acquainted with their shared history or why he chose her as his main competitor.

"Do you have the records of your time in foster care?" he asked. "There will be people listed who you may not remember being in your life at that time."

"I put a call into the parish family services agency. They're working on getting my file over to me." She stepped closer to the photographs, map and timeline they'd posted on the board. "I asked they bring it by the end of the day. I don't remember everyone who was in and out of my life back then. Truth be told, I blocked out a lot of my childhood."

He checked the time. They'd blown through lunch and the task force would meet soon. On a narrow table pushed against the wall, two fast-food bags with two cups sat neglected. Someone must have brought them food at some point. Could have even mentioned it but he and Charlotte had been so hyper-focused that neither had noticed.

He unfolded the top of one of the bags, pulled out a wrapped burger and took it over to Charlotte along with a drink. "Take a break and eat something. You'll be leading the task force meeting in ten minutes."

She licked her lips. With a groan, she unwrapped the hamburger then took a bite. "I forgot what food tastes like."

Austin followed her example. But instead of Charlotte's controlled pace, he scarfed his burger down in a few bites. Once he was done eating, he took a moment to tidy the boxes, files and paperwork that had been scattered on the conference table.

"I forgot what a neat freak you are." She stood at the door, her laptop tucked underneath her arm. "Ready to go?"

Before following her out, Austin took a minute to look at the photographs of the four victims. He would put up one of Ginny Gerard as soon as they received the photo from her family. "You have not been forgotten." He spoke to the murdered women like they were standing in the room. In his mind and heart, they were. "Your killer will face justice for what he did." He turned his gaze to the picture of Ruby, whose resemblance to Charlotte was striking. "And I promise to keep Charlotte safe."

With notebook and pen in hand, he turned off the lights and left the room, locking the door behind him, securing the proof of stolen lives.

Charlotte left the first Presque Killer task force meeting more hopeful than she'd been before. The boost of personnel would keep the investigation moving at the fast pace required. For his part, Austin stayed in the background, his hands loosely clasped behind him. She'd learned from working with him years ago that he preferred to observe rather than talk. His quiet demeanor and relaxed expression hid a federal law enforcement professional who did not miss even the slightest detail. While the meeting was progressing and different personnel were sharing their opinions about the course of the investigation, Charlotte could almost hear the gears turning in Austin's head. Anticipation grew to hear his thoughts and gather his opinion on how best to use the resources the task force provided.

She unlocked the door to the conference room and stepped inside. Everything was how they'd left it. Not that she suspected a police officer of being the killer but the first thing that Austin had taught her when he'd arrived six years ago was that when hunting a serial killer, no one was ruled out automatically. No one got a free pass because of their job or who they were in the community.

A knock startled her out of her ruminations. "Detective Reid, a reporter from the newspaper is here to see you."

"Who?" Not that she had time for any of them but one local reporter in particular always raised her defenses.

"Ronald Rheault," Gladys, the woman who worked at the front desk, said. "He isn't taking no for an answer."

"He never does." At least when it came to stories involving the Presque Police Department and more specifically Charlotte Reid.

"What do you what me to tell him? Go away?" Gladys smiled. She had a motherly air about her that made Charlotte long for a mother who was still alive and had not been arrested and taken away.

"I'll talk to him," she said with resignation. "A few no comments and then send him on his way."

On her way to the front, she passed by Austin, who'd stayed behind after the meeting to talk with the state detective charged with investigating last night's kidnapping.

"Where are you headed?" he asked, pivoting to face her. "Not leaving without me?"

"Wouldn't dream of it." Warmth filled her chest. Normally, she pushed away any gesture of overprotection. Charlotte had a badge and a gun and a smart brain. She didn't need anyone, specially men, falling over themselves to keep her safe. But Austin's concern hit differently. Most likely due to the killer's direct threat to her.

She carried on down the hallway and exited into the lobby. Ronald had positioned himself at the front desk as if daring anyone to ask him to leave without getting what he came for. "Mr. Rheault, how may I help you?"

He jumped slightly at the sound of her voice in the otherwise quiet lobby. Turning to face her, he met her gaze.

A fleeting expression passed over his face that Charlotte couldn't identify but she sensed he'd concealed his true feelings.

"Detective." Ronald cleared his throat. "I'm writing a story on the reemergence of the Presque Killer. And since you haven't held a press conference yet, I'm here in person to get answers. How is the investigation going? Do you have any solid leads? What does the presence of an FBI agent mean in regards to the department's faith in your abilities?"

She ground her teeth and took another step toward him. "Those are a lot of questions."

"Only three." He flipped open a spiral notebook then took a pencil off its resting spot on his ear. "Let's start with suspects. Do you have any?"

"No comment." Keeping her facial expression neutral was difficult when she faced an annoying reporter. Actually, Ronald Rheault was more than annoying. He'd been downright intrusive during the last Presque Killer investigation. She didn't expect preferential treatment from the local media but he'd printed speculations and not facts after the murder of Ruby. Charlotte had never gotten over her irritation.

"Okay." Ronald made an act of writing in his notebook while wearing a smirk. "The FBI agent you're working with, is he the same one as last time?"

"Special Agent Walsh has returned to assist." Maybe a crumb would satisfy him.

"Has the FBI taken over the investigation?"

Her temper was rising by the question. *Stay calm. He wants to see a reaction.* "No comment."

"Is there anything you want to comment on for the

story?" Ronald arched an eyebrow. "You've accused me of misrepresenting your work in previous stories."

"Don't write fiction and I won't have a problem." She turned her head in a signal her tolerance was almost gone.

Ronald jotted down some more notes before closing his notebook. "I'm covering this story, whether you talk to me or not. I have other sources in the department. I've lived in Presque most of my life, which means I know most of the people in the town. Went to school with many, including you."

That comment captured her attention. She studied him closely, not dismissing the reporter anymore. "That's right, we were in the same grade for a few years, until I changed schools. I forgot."

"Of course you did." He snorted, shaking his head. "Charlotte Reid, always keeping everyone at a distance. With your sister being the only exception. Let me know if you want to share any facts with the public. They have a right to know."

She stood frozen in the lobby until Ronald left the building. A scrawny news reporter was not a serial killer. Half the town had known her at some point during her youth.

But she couldn't rule anyone out. She'd ask an officer to discreetly look into Ronald's recent whereabouts just in case. If anything, to rule him out.

While she was still in the lobby, a social services worker entered. The worker had brought over Charlotte's file from her years in the system. She'd been kind enough to print out the documents. Charlotte found examining paper documents easier than clicking around on a computer screen. Plus, she and Austin could share the task of looking over each one.

After thanking the worker for the quick delivery, Charlotte held the folder tight to her chest. *God, guide us to the person harming Your children. Use me for Your purposes.*

She strode down the hallway, back to the conference room and Austin. The time had come to take a looking glass to her history. The clues they'd been searching for might be buried in her past.

SEVEN

Charlotte rubbed her eyes and yawned. She and Austin had recorded the names and address of the six foster homes she and Ruby had resided in along with various foster children and families whom they'd shared a home with.

She was running criminal histories on everyone she'd listed. If she got a hit and their DNA had been logged into the system, she placed them on a "not likely" list. The one piece of trace evidence they had ruled out anyone who'd been arrested for a number of specific types of crimes. Each state's DNA collection laws varied, which made a broad search a little harder to use for eliminating suspects.

"We can rule out females, which removes about fifty percent of the people who touched your life during foster care." Austin glanced up from his laptop screen with his reading glasses perched on the tip of his nose. "You're confident the person who abducted you was a man, right?"

"Yes, even though he used something to alter his voice, it was male. Aren't most serial killers men?"

"Most but not all." He pushed his reading glasses back onto the bridge of his nose. "In these cases, a female suspect would be highly unlikely."

The fluttery feeling in her stomach produced by the intensity of his gaze was the reason she'd fallen for him. And his good looks were only magnified when he wore glasses. Why did her attraction to the dedicated FBI special agent resurface when all her concentration should be on catching a killer? She could not be distracted by the thick lashes framing Austin's eyes or the way the corners of his mouth turned down while absorbed in a task. Not again. The murdered women deserved every ounce of her attention. Meaning she'd reinforce their professional boundaries.

After enough time had passed, she could admit he'd broken her heart when he left six years ago. Why had Austin been the one man who'd smashed the protective walls around her heart? She'd known from the start he'd never be permanent.

Charlotte returned her attention to the list of names. One jumped out along with a couple of disturbing memories. Michael Duncan had struck her as strange on the first day she'd met him. Michael had a brief stay in the White household during the time Charlotte had lived there. She'd been about thirteen at the time. While Michael had lived with the foster family for only a short while, those months had been scary for the entire group living in the house.

"Michael Duncan," she said to Austin, "was a resident at a home I lived in with Ruby until he threatened to kill Mrs. White. He was sent to a group home after that."

"Where does he live now?" Austin stood behind her and gazed over her shoulder at the information Charlotte viewed.

She typed in Michael Duncan with his date of birth in the search fields of the database. Within seconds, pages of Michael's life history appeared on the screen. "No arrests and no criminal history. He's lived at the same address for ten years. His house is in Presque, on the south side of town. No wife or children listed."

"Have you had any interactions with him since you

lived together in foster care?" Austin scanned the computer screen, taking his own notes.

"I'd need to see how he looks to know for certain." She flipped through her memory. "I'm sure I've come across him given that we both live in the same town."

"We should pay him a visit." Austin checked his watch, and his eyes widened. "It's after ten already. I should send in a report to my supervisor."

The mention of contacting his supervisor produced a flash of fear. At any point, Austin could be pulled off the case for a second time for a higher priority case, and she had no doubt he'd follow orders. Charlotte glanced outside and for the first time noticed the darkness. "No wonder I'm so tired. I can't afford to sleep. At least not until the killer is off the street."

"You'll need to rest in order to function." He pulled back her chair and assisted her to stand. "Go home and sleep. We'll pay a visit to Mr. Duncan first thing tomorrow morning."

She arched her low back, stretching the tight muscles. "I can't stop yet. There are a few more people I need to check into." Especially if she might lose Austin's help at the word of someone hundreds of miles away.

The sound of footsteps preceded the entrance of Officer Kagan. A youthful eagerness shone on his face. "I spoke with Ronald Rheault about his whereabouts last night around the time the waitress was kidnapped."

Charlotte groaned. "I don't want him thinking he's a suspect."

"Who's Ronald Rheault?" Austin asked, glancing back and forth between Charlotte and Officer Kagan.

"He's a reporter for the local newspaper," she answered. "You may remember him from our last investigation. Tall, skinny guy with a way of showing up everywhere he's not wanted."

"Sounds vaguely familiar." Austin removed his reading glasses and set them on a stack of papers on the table. "Why are you checking on his alibi for when the kidnapping occurred?"

"He showed up at the station this afternoon, asking questions, which is his job," she answered. How to explain the sense of unease she'd experienced around him? Could be she was suspicious of everyone crossing her path who fit the killer's profile. A reporter's job was to chase a story, and one as big as the Presque Killer garnered national media attention. Charlotte didn't find it odd that the local news was desperate for an inside scoop. But something about Ronald in particular caused an extra dose of wariness. Even during the prior investigation, she'd gotten the impression he wasn't focused on the news story but instead some of his interest was directed on her. "I get a weird vibe with him," she continued. "And a job as a reporter could be a good cover for someone wanting to commit crimes then stay informed about the investigation."

"What did you find?" Austin asked the officer.

Office Kagan's posture straightened. "Don't worry, I made up a story of why I wanted to know where Ronald was last evening. I told him a strange man was seen lurking outside his house. I played it cool so he wouldn't tie my questions to the kidnapping."

She didn't want to burst the young officer's bubble by disagreeing. The news reporter had likely seen right through his story. Only ten years ago, she'd been filled with youthful ambition, striving to impress her superiors. Working for a small-town police department, she'd started out naive, much like Officer Kagan. She hoped the younger officer didn't make some of the same mistakes she had. Looking back, she wished she'd done some things differently. Falling in love with her FBI partner being top of the list.

"Did Ronald have an alibi?" she asked since Officer Kagan failed to provide the most crucial part of the story on his own.

"Not really. He said he was home asleep. He lives alone and parks his car in the garage."

"Would he have access to a box truck?" Austin took out photos of the scene by the café and pointed at the tire tracks found next to the victim's van.

"The newspaper has one," Charlotte replied. "Kagan, I'm sure your shift ended a while ago." Just as hers had. "Tomorrow morning go by the newspaper office and see if they can account for their truck and find out who has access to the keys. Who knows, it may morph into a lead."

Office Kagan gave a sharp nod. "Yes, ma'am. First thing in the morning."

Charlotte cringed at the use of *ma'am*. No matter how many times she asked to be addressed as detective instead of ma'am, she couldn't break the Southern habit that had been ingrained in generations of schoolboys and girls. "Thank you, Officer. Good night."

"Time to take your own advice." Austin organized the piles of reports, files and random papers, once again, then placed his belongings into his messenger bag. He checked his phone. "I have a missed call from my supervisor. He's likely looking for my report. I should call him back before I leave."

Her stomach clenched in speculation. *Please God, keep him here until I see this through.*

Austin followed Charlotte home after convincing her to halt their research for the day. Actually the day was almost over. Only fifteen more minutes until midnight. According to the killer's deadline, they had six more days to find him. Six days. Not nearly enough time but Austin prayed the killer would be identified and arrested well before the countdown ended.

The blinker on Charlotte's car flashed red and then she turned onto her street. She lived in a nice part of town, with well-kept homes and mature trees providing shade during these hot summer days.

When she pulled into her driveway, he parked on the street. Tonight, he would drop the act and get out of the car before she disappeared into the house. He was certain she'd seen him yesterday, walking around her property in a security sweep.

Charlotte left her car in the unattached garage, lowered the garage door, then waved at Austin, who stood in the driveway like a bouncer at a club. "See you tomorrow."

"Try to get some sleep and don't forget to eat." He didn't want her to think him a hovering mother but he understood too well the cumulative effects murder cases had on a person's body. An investigator who skipped meals and worked all hours of the day often crashed and burned, eventually being sidelined. The last time he'd teamed up with Charlotte, he'd seen the early signs of burnout. And then the murder of her sister had flipped a switch. Her drive had turned superhuman. Though no amount of hours worked or determination had resulted in a viable suspect and an arrest. *Work smarter not harder*, Caleb used to say. The man had been full of clever sayings. Austin needed his mentor's wisdom now more than ever.

"Austin," Charlotte called out as she approached the back door. "Someone broke in."

Hand resting on his gun, he rushed to where she stood,

three feet back from the concrete steps to the door, which had been left ajar. "Are you sure you closed and locked it when you left? You were in a rush after you got the missing persons call."

"I'm positive." She removed her gun from the holster on her hip. "And if I had, my neighbor would call. She's eighty and her kitchen window overlooks this side of my house."

Austin crept forward, gun gripped in his hand. Pointing the tip of the gun forward, he pushed open the door with his foot.

"I'm right behind you," Charlotte whispered. "Calling for backup."

He entered a quiet house; only the light above the kitchen sink provided illumination. No movement caught his eye.

"I'll take the second story. You search down here." She waited for Austin's nod of confirmation before tiptoeing toward the staircase.

After exploring each room on the ground floor for signs of human disturbance, either past or present, he returned to the kitchen. All clear, at least on this level. The sound of a muffler backfiring from outside made him jump. He ran out and down the driveway. A half block down, a white pickup truck sped away and turned the corner, soon out of sight. The distance was too great for him to make out the license plate.

"What was that?" Charlotte asked in a breathless voice. "It sounded like a gunshot."

"A muffler backfired, and the truck raced off." He surveyed the neighborhood. Besides a dog barking nearby, all remained peaceful.

"Come back inside. Whoever was here left me a gift." Her face paled in the low light of the street lamps. The circles under her eyes seemed to have deepened to the shade of thunderclouds.

Austin returned into her house, keeping watch. "The first floor was clear."

"Same with the second." She waved him up the stairs, then guided him into her bedroom. "There's a note. I haven't touched it."

Dread spiraled. A note card lay on the center of her bed. Normally, a white card with a few words written on its surface wouldn't seem menacing. But by now he knew that script and whom it belonged to.

One hundred forty-four hours until you are mine

The Presque Killer had invaded Charlotte's home. Her bedroom. They were playing his sick game. Why the taunts? What purpose did it serve other than to boost the killer's ego? A lack of respect from others was a common propellant for men in particular to start killing. The man they were chasing possessed a strong need to validate his superiority. Austin considered how the killer's recent behavior modified the profile he'd created. An overexaggerated sense of self indicated a period in the killer's life when he'd suffered poor self-esteem. Childhood, perhaps. The killer had felt overlooked, or others had perhaps actively mocked him.

He planned to visit Michael Duncan, the man who'd once lived with Charlotte and her sister in foster care, and Austin would get a good opportunity to read him and learn if he fit the profile.

He checked out the window to find an empty street. "Backup response needs to be quicker."

"I know but the department only has two officers on duty most night shifts. They could be attending to another situation." She shivered. "It makes me sick that he was in my house, in my bedroom."

Austin called Chief Gunther, rousing him from sleep. As expected, the chief promised to come as soon as he changed.

"You should find somewhere else to stay." After Charlotte left the bedroom, he switched off the light. "Is there a friend you could live with until we catch this guy?"

"I can't put anyone in danger." She gripped the handrail and descended the stairs with care. "One hundred forty-four hours." Her feet touched the landing, then she halted. "Time is moving fast."

He took hold of her elbow and walked alongside her into the kitchen. After seating her on a chair at the table, he poured her a glass of water and handed it over. The stress was taking its toll. If they didn't stop the killer, women would die, including Charlotte.

"He's taking chances this time he didn't before. He's growing bold." Austin poured a glass of water for himself and took a long drink. The cool liquid quenched a thirst he wasn't aware he had. "He will slip up, if he hasn't already. Making the chase personal informs us that he knows you deeper than only as the detective assigned to find and arrest him, and coming here, into your house, tells me that success made him less cautious."

"The truck that sped away could have been him. Did you see the make and model or get a license plate number?"

He wished he'd gotten a better look. But wishes didn't solve cases. He worked with the facts available and used logic to build from there. "A white pickup truck. An older model, judging from the muffler backfire."

"Of course, a white truck." She shook her head. "Half

the population around here has a white truck, or at least that's what it seems."

"One of your neighbors may have seen something." With a good enough view to make an identification. If only they could get so lucky.

"A possibility." A knock at the back door jolted her.

Austin answered and found two police officers had arrived. He let them in. Soon, Chief Gunther marched in, appearing angry and concerned.

"Your house is a crime scene, Detective." The chief's tone of voice left no room for argument. "Pack what you'll need for a few days. On second thought, you're not coming home until this situation has ended."

"I don't have family left and even if I did, I wouldn't ask them to stay. My presence puts others in danger." She pushed to her feet and forcefully brushed her hand across the top of her head. "I can't stand that the killer is winning."

"Not for long." Austin stepped in front of her to stop her from pacing. "You're coming to the Magnolia Hotel with me. You can get a room next to mine." At the sight of the scowl on her face, he pressed his lips together. "The hotel isn't that bad, really. The muffins in the lobby are tasty."

"Fine." She stomped off. The pounding of footsteps up above meant bags were being packed.

"I'll sleep better knowing you're close by." Chief Gunther tipped his chin to gaze at the ceiling. "Don't take her bluster personally. She's furious but not with you."

"The killer left her a note." Could he have been careless enough to leave fingerprints on the card stock? They'd know as soon as tomorrow morning. The task force included a dedicated team of forensic technicians to gather and process the growing collection of evidence left by the Presque Killer's actions.

"I'd love to send him a note." Chief Gunther pounded his fist on the counter. "Mine will be the first one he receives in jail."

The chief might have to fight Charlotte for that privilege.

But what if they failed again? The killer had promised to kill Charlotte. He believed he'd win the sick game he'd created and then disappear. Temporary doubt blinded Austin to all other outcomes.

No. He shook off the panic. This time was different. Good would prevail and evil would fall. He'd continue to lift up prayers to God, who promised to bring justice to the wicked.

EIGHT

The next morning, Charlotte startled awake. *Where am I?* She sat upright, and her groggy mind struggled to make sense of her surroundings.

The Magnolia Hotel. That was why it smelled of air freshener and stale air. She fell back and rested her head on the pillow. Austin was right, the hotel wasn't as bad as she'd expected. A relatively clean room and a comfortable bed. She'd need to remember to turn on the air conditioner before she left to drive away the humidity in the room. The best part, though—the reassurance that Austin was only steps away. Sleep had caught her fast after she'd checked in and gotten settled. Surprising, since her stress level had been as high as a rocket ready to burst through the earth's atmosphere.

She checked the time and wondered if Austin was up yet. Knowing the tireless FBI agent, he'd probably only slept a few hours and was drinking coffee while reviewing all the notes he'd scribbled down in his always-present notebook.

What would her life look like once the killer was locked away? Of course, she'd still be single, returning home every day after work to an empty house. Living until the age of eight with a mom who specialized in dysfunctional relationships then being tossed around in foster care did not provide a roadmap for a happy-ever-after. Charlotte had accepted long ago that trusting a man enough to love him with her whole heart and soul was too great a risk. The one time she'd let down her guard, believing God sent a man into her life worthy of her faith, had proven nothing good came from romantic love. Austin was a good man but his leaving had shown her that the pain she'd witnessed in her mom had been real. Charlotte had endured enough abandonment to last ten lifetimes. Only a fool would open herself to more. After Austin left, he'd moved on. She had not. Solving the Presque cases had become her life.

Her brain was struck by a jolt—a reminder why she was here at the hotel and not home. The Presque Killer had broken into her house. She jumped out of bed. No time to lie around and mourn her failed romantic life.

Once showered and dressed, she holstered her gun then unlocked the door, checking for threats before fully opening it. The only threat she found was the one to her heart. Austin stood on the walkway outside her door with a small bag in one hand and a tray with two cups of coffee in the other.

"Breakfast." He said with a grin. "The hotel doesn't have real room service, so you'll have to make do with me."

She'd never consider Austin a *less than* option. He was the best there was, as an FBI special agent and at delivering breakfast. "Come in." Stepping aside, she waited for him to enter then shut the door. "I checked the vehicles registered to Michael Duncan last night," she said. "He owns a white truck."

"As you said yesterday, most of the men in Kingston Parish own white trucks. Eat first. Then we'll dig further into Mr. Duncan and pay him a visit." Austin pulled out two muffins and napkins from the bag.

Her appetite remained weak but she knew Austin would

not let her leave without eating. She grabbed a muffin and took a bite. *"Mmm..."* she hummed. "These are good. Orange cranberry, correct?"

"That's what the sign said." Austin downed his muffin with only a few bites. "This hotel really is the best place for you. I ran into about a half dozen task force members from out of town who are staying here as well. The killer'd be crazy to attempt anything here."

"The killer is crazy, remember?" Even with food inside, her stomach growled, asking for more. She really should remember to eat on a regular basis throughout the days ahead, even if she didn't feel like it. Chasing criminals required strength. With her muffin devoured, she opened the lid of her steaming coffee and took a cautious first sip.

With her free hand, she powered up her laptop. "Here is the most recent driver's license photo of Michael Duncan." A man with closely cropped brown hair and pockmarked skin glared back on the screen. "He has a sealed record as a minor. I'd need a warrant to read it."

"Right now, we don't have anything to show a judge that supports a warrant request." He removed his reading glasses from the front pocket of his crisp white dress shirt and put them on to study the photograph. "What do you remember about him from your time together? Did you see him after he left the foster home?"

"All I can recall are the feelings of panic whenever I was around him. He didn't have a nice bone in his body, and I believe he enjoyed the fear he saw in the other kids and our foster parents. He felt powerful making others feel weak."

"His childhood personality matches the path of a future serial killer but not all bullies grow up to kill people," he said. "What about after he was removed from the home?

Did you ever run into him around town?" Austin tapped on the screen, indicating the face of the man.

"I'm not sure." She shook her head, frustrated with her lack of memory. "Presque isn't a big town and it's likely our paths have crossed. Any interaction doesn't stand out. Wait." She leaned closer to get a better look at the tattoo on Michael's neck—an inked image of a spider hanging down from a crescent moon. "I remember this tattoo. Years ago, I was at a restaurant with Ruby. He approached our table and acted offended we didn't know him. He even tried to sit at our booth next to Ruby. I'd wondered at the time if he was one of her druggie friends she didn't want to acknowledge in front of me. He ended up leaving, never telling us how he knew us."

"Instead of one of Ruby's friends, he was someone who'd lived with you both in foster care for a short period of time." He removed his glasses, then took a long drink of coffee. "I'm ready to make a house call whenever you are."

"Let's roll." She put on her badge, which she hung from a chain around her neck, then checked her service weapon. "Do you think we'll need backup?"

"I don't want to spook him. I'll let the chief know where we're going. The task force is meeting at ten, so we have two hours to talk with Mr. Duncan."

Nerves fluttered in Charlotte's chest. The memories involving Michael Duncan still produced fear. Speaking with suspects was nothing new. Going to the home of the potential Presque Killer, a man who'd lingered as a dark storm over the area for six long years, couldn't be approached carelessly.

Austin drove, which allowed Charlotte time to write down questions and word each in a way to elicit the best response. He located the address, a run-down clapboard house set up on cement blocks, and parked on the street. No vehicle could be seen in the driveway. Once out of the SUV, Austin moved to get a better view down the long driveway. He saw no garage. Could be no one was home.

Charlotte took the lead, heading up the rickety stairs and onto the front porch. A worn-out lawn chair was surrounded by cigarette butts and empty beer cans scattered on the porch floor. She gave three sharp knocks on the frame of the screen door and stepped back. After no answer, she knocked again. "Either he's not home or he's hiding."

Austin's head turned toward the direction of the street to the sight of a white truck driving in their direction. The driver pulled into the driveway, stopping beside the house.

A man exited, with a cigarette dangling from his lips and a hard-sided cooler gripped in one hand. "What are you doing here?" The scowl on his face deepened the lines around his mouth and did not appear the least bit welcoming. However, he didn't act surprised to see them.

"FBI Special Agent Walsh." Austin showed his identification and badge. "This is Detective Reid with the Presque Police Department."

"I know who you are." He pointed a thick finger at Charlotte. "I asked what you're doing on my front porch."

"We're investigating a recent murder and kidnapping," Charlotte said.

He stared at her with narrowed eyes, which were bloodshot. "That has nothing to do with me."

During the initial interaction, Austin made a quick study of Michael Duncan. His defensive demeanor produced suspicion. But that behavior was normal when FBI and police showed up unannounced at a person's home. He appeared like he was coming home from work, suggesting he worked third shift. A computer search of the property deed showed the house he resided in was owned by his birth mother. If she lived with her son, who had been removed from her care at some point, how was their relationship now?

Austin focused his gaze on the tattoo peeking out from underneath the collar of Michael's shirt. The spider, though it appeared menacing, didn't catch his interest. But the crescent moon, the shape that had been carved into the arms of the victims, held his gaze. What was the symbolism of a crescent moon, and how did it tie back to the Presque Killer?

"Where were you the last three evenings?" Charlotte inquired. Her body language suggested a simple question. Austin knew the strain she was hiding on the inside.

Michael huffed and marched toward the front door. "I was at work. If you think I had anything to do with those girls, you're wrong."

"Mr. Duncan, we're looking into people with a shared connection to Detective Reid." Austin projected calm and confidence. Like Charlotte, he didn't want Michael to realize the depth of their interest. "Do you remember the detective from when you were in foster care?"

Michael's body froze with one foot on the bottom porch step. He swung around, still clutching the cooler. The cigarette in his mouth had been reduced to a small stub. He plucked it out and ground the remainder under the sole of his work boot. "I remember every day of that living hell." He clenched his jaw. "You were at the White home when I got there. Do-gooder family thought dragging us poor foster kids to church would save our souls. My soul was too long gone by that time." His gaze returned to Charlotte, intensifying. "You were there with your little sister. Both of you looked ready to jump out of your skin at the slightest word." He snickered. "But I never hurt nobody. Not back then and not now."

Charlotte descended the stairs to stand on the front lawn, which was covered in more dirt than grass. Scattered litter added an extra layer to the appearance of neglect. She stepped over a rusted child's tricycle and moved closer to where Michael stood by the stairs. "Where do you work?"

"I don't have to answer your questions." He jutted out his chin. "And I could tell you to get off my property."

"Your mom's property," Austin corrected. He scanned the ground to see if anything had writing that he could compare to the killer's handwriting. Nothing so far. "And yes, you could. But that wouldn't help us clear you."

"You think I did those things?" Michael's face reddened. "Except for some trouble I got into as a kid, I've never been arrested for anything. Never in jail. Are you suspecting every former foster kid or just me?" He hooked a thumb at his chest.

"Not just you." Charlotte kept her voice even, not giving in to the rising tension. "But if you answer our questions, we'll be on our way and you can get back to whatever you were going to do."

"Sleep," he spit out. "I work nights at Southern Healthcare Laundry Service. When I get home after a shift, all I want to do is have a beer and go to sleep."

Austin added the name of the business in his notes. "What do you do there?"

"Pickup and delivery. I pick up dirty linens from the area hospitals and bring them to the washing facility. Then I deliver carts of the clean linens back to the hospitals." He set the cooler on the step. "I'm a solid worker. Call my boss if you'd like. He'll tell you I've been working every night since Monday. They don't have enough drivers, so I'm on about sixty hours a week."

Michael was a driver, meaning he traveled the streets of Presque and the surrounding areas, alone in a work truck. Would he have been able to get his personal truck and visit Charlotte's house last night during his work shift? "Where is your work facility located?"

"Off Valor Road, by the old furniture manufacturer plant." Michael plucked out another cigarette from the packet stuffed in the front pocket of his T-shirt and lit up.

Austin had no idea how far that location was to Charlotte's house. A question for later. "Have you ever had any run-ins with Detective Reid recently? Any hard feelings?"

Michael's narrowed eyed gaze swung from Austin to Charlotte. The manner in which Michael looked at her, like he had secret knowledge about her, made Austin uneasy.

"I learned real quick that some people figure they're too good for you, even if y'all came from the same place." Michael directed his comment at Charlotte. "You and your sister didn't want nothing to do with any of us, even after we're all grown. After Ruby was killed, I felt sorry for you cause you had nobody."

Austin's instincts to protect Charlotte clashed with his professional obligation to let this interaction play out. Witnessing Michael's unguarded emotions could break open the case and help them find the killer. But seeing Charlotte's pale face and pain-filled large brown eyes hurt his heart. It wasn't fair that Charlotte had to relive her childhood trauma in an attempt to bring the killer to justice. The killer had pointed them down this path, and Austin asked God for the strength to finish the race.

NINE

You had nobody. With a sharp intake of breath, Charlotte took a small step backward, away from the words spoken with the intent to pierce her like a bullet. She steadied her emotions, fitted armor around her heart. This man would not catch her off-balance. "Did you know my sister, Ruby? As an adult, I mean."

He shrugged and shook his head, in contradiction. "Not really."

"Not really or no?" She pressed. "Ruby liked to party. I thought perhaps you both ran in the same circles."

"I'd see her from time to time." Michael drew a long pull of his cigarette. "Ruby knew how to have fun, unlike her big sister. Your enjoyment, Officer, only came from busting up a party."

A cough tickled in the back of her throat. The smoke from the cigarette aggravated her airways. It also brought flashbacks of Charlotte's time living with her mom, who'd chain-smoked since high school. The smell of cigarette smoke brought both good and painful memories. Her mom hadn't been all bad. She'd tried her best to provide love, food and a roof over their heads. Granted, most of her attempts at financial stability were illegal. A single mother with few resources. Finally, her crimes had earned her a jail sentence. Jail hadn't been kind to a childlike spirt like her mom, and the confinement had killed her.

Charlotte fixed her gaze on the tattoo on his neck, and a memory rattled loose. He'd stolen Charlotte's crescent moon bracelet while they'd lived together and then taunted her when she begged for its return. Only as Michael was being taken to the group home did she get it back. "When was the last time you saw Ruby?" she asked in a voice void of emotion. Charlotte could not let Michael know how much he'd disturbed her.

Austin's close proximity was the glue that kept her reactions in check. They made a great team. Too bad she didn't believe he'd stick around any longer than needed to get the job done. Next case. Next town. Next partner. And once again, she'd be a memory.

Michael remained silent, passively refusing to answer.

"Did you see Ruby around the time of her murder?" Austin asked again with a touch more force.

"I don't have to answer you." Michael scowled. "Girls like Ruby don't matter." He gestured to Austin. "The detective only cares because it's her sister who was killed. The poor and addicted get passed over by society all the time. A few go missing. A few are found dead. Who cares, right? Not the police."

"I care about every one of those women," Charlotte spit out, too enraged to fake control.

"Then good luck. You'll need it." Michael flicked the remainder of his second cigarette at the ground by Austin's feet, almost hitting the tip of his leather shoe. "You have any more questions, then call my lawyer." He chuckled. "I'm going inside to get some sleep." The slap of the screen door closing provided the final punctuation in his closing statement.

"What do you think?" She asked Austin.

His gaze was directed down at his feet. After going to his car and returning with gloves and an evidence collection bag, he slipped on the gloves and leaned over. Pinching the still smoldering cigarette butt in between his thumb and pointer finger, he studied it then motioned her to follow him to his vehicle. "I think we have a DNA sample," he said once they were a safe distance from the house. "Do you think the Presque Killer would be so careless with his DNA?"

She considered. "Sure, if he didn't know we have the killer's DNA on file from the first murder victim. That piece of information wasn't released to the public and only those in the tight circle of investigation know."

They stood on the sidewalk, waiting for the cigarette to cool in order to place it inside the plastic bag. While waiting, she scrutinized the house and what she'd learned about Michael Duncan. He still possessed the meanness she'd experienced from him as a child. A hard life would do that to a person. But not all those who experienced difficult childhoods killed for sport. No, something more sinister had taken root in a person's heart to compel him to snuff the life out of others. Did Michael Duncan's spiteful words mask something wicked and cruel? Or was he like so many other men she'd interacted with, especially in her line of work, who bullied and intimidated as a means of releasing their anger and frustration?

Austin dropped the cigarette butt into the evidence bag and sealed the top. "This will go to the state forensics lab with a rush order." He'd turned his back to the house, hiding the treasure he'd collected from anyone watching from inside.

"We'll either get a match or we can rule him out." She

rubbed her temples. "The results will take too long to come back. I need them now."

They got into the car, and Austin started the engine. "My gut tells me Michael Duncan isn't our killer. His temper makes him quick to snap. In contrast, the Presque Killer is calculating and methodical."

"Could be an act." Charlotte turned to view the house as they drove away, catching a glimpse of a man standing at the window before the curtain dropped.

"It's a possibility. The killer we're hunting is cunning." He flipped the turn signal and directed the SUV back to the police station. "A smart person can wear a different personality while interacting with the public to hide who he really is. A sociopath has to learn from an early age to blend in."

She dwelled on what Michael had said about Ruby and herself. Did people in the town really believe law enforcement didn't care about women like Ruby? Did they speculate to one another that the murder cases had gone cold because no one cared enough to keep fighting for the truth? The idea brought tears to Charlotte's eyes. If only people understood how many hours she and other officers had dedicated to catching the killer even before her sister became a victim. She'd lived and breathed those cases. Even after her resources were pulled and the files were ordered into storage, she'd kept the fire of the investigation burning, unofficially.

"Hey." Austin reached over and rested a hand over Charlotte's hand, which was placed on her lap. "I can hear your thoughts. Don't let that guy convince you that people in the town don't know how deeply you care about solving these murders."

"Do they?" Her voice cracked while asking the question. "Some people blame me and the department for six years of no results. Women were murdered. They were sisters and daughters, and their families deserve answers. I can't bring back their loved ones but I should bring the person who murdered them to justice."

Alarm built at the realization of the truth. Having been blinded by her own grief and frustration, she'd failed to comprehend the feelings of the community. She heard their voices in her head, crashing into her all at once.

"I've worked enough of these types of cases to understand that no matter what you do or what happens, the people affected don't have a happy outcome." He squeezed her hand before returning his to the steering wheel. "How can they, with no sense of control other than to talk? Some families hire private investigators or start asking questions, but even if the killer is caught and convicted, it's a shallow victory. The death remains. They still no longer have their loved one."

Charlotte heard what Austin was saying and the intention behind his words. All she could think about was these murders in her community and that they remained unsolved for so many years. And if she failed to catch the killer by the end of his deadline, then more deaths would occur. More loved ones would grieve.

"I want to hold a press conference. The chief so far has only allowed press releases." The idea firmed in her head. "It's the only way to keep the public informed and maybe we'll get a lead. I want people to know we're not sitting on our hands."

"That's a good idea." Once they arrived at the police station, Austin found an open spot in the parking lot. He shut off the SUV and turned in his seat to face her. The corners of his mouth curved down with concern. "A press conference may shake loose some new information. Don't let anything Michael Duncan said get under your skin. If he is the Presque Killer, his intention was to further taunt you. And if he's innocent, then he's an example of a bitter man who's lived a hard life without love."

She took several deep breaths, in and out. Austin was right. The Presque Killer delighted in bringing her low, building fear and observing the destruction he created. Her mind needed to stop spinning and refocus on the investigation. The more emotion took over, the blurrier the facts appeared. *Be more like Austin. Use logic to gaze from a distance, and the pieces of the puzzle might come into focus.*

The conference room hummed with energy, which Charlotte used to feed her spirit. She stood at the head of the table and glanced at the men and women filling the room. All professionals in the investigative and law enforcement fields. A representative from the crime lab was present. Austin had entered the cigarette butt into evidence and handed it over to be processed. Could it really be that easy? Get a DNA match and arrest Michael Duncan as the Presque Killer?

She had an officer contacting the laundry where Mr. Duncan worked in order to verify he'd been on duty the nights Ginny Gerard and Karen Tremont went missing. Although, even if he had been working, if he'd driven the routes alone with no GPS tracker on his truck, any short side trips would go unnoticed. She also requested the make and model of the truck he drove in case it matched the tire tracks found beside Karen's van.

Charlotte cleared her throat, indicating it was time to start. "Thank you everyone for accepting the assignment to come to Presque and assist with the investigation. I realize most of you have left family at home to be here, and your sacrifice does not go unnoticed." She paused to take a drink of water. Nerves dried her mouth like pavement under a hot sun. "I'd like to start with each team reporting on their findings so far, bringing everyone up to date. Special Agent Walsh and I will cover what we've learned over the last few days and discuss the pertinent facts of the cold cases."

A rumble of agreement spurred her to continue. The sight of Austin boosted her confidence. She'd never led a group this large, with so many talented professionals. The killer's short time frame had sent the investigation into overdrive.

"Unfortunately no evidence has been recovered from my kidnapping a few days ago. Let's start with the kidnapping of Karen Tremont. Any new leads or pieces of information?" she asked the pair of Kingston Parish detectives seated nearby. During the last investigation, the parish investigators had shown no motivation to solve the murders of drug-addicted young women. Charlotte got a different vibe from the two from the parish today. They seemed eager to bring the killer to justice.

"A cast was made of the tire tracks found by Mrs. Tremont's van," a woman with auburn hair said. She wore a red short-sleeve shirt. "The imprint matches a brand of tires found on Freightliner medium duty box trucks. Axle to axle is eighteen feet. We searched trucks with tires matching the tracks and found several registered to different businesses in the area."

"Is Southern Healthcare Laundry Service on that list?" Austin asked.

The female investigator checked the sheet on the table, scanning it until she reached the bottom. "Yes, they own two of the same model. Why do you ask?"

"A potential suspect works there." Austin glanced at

Charlotte, and his gaze locked on hers. "There's a chance he drives one of those trucks."

"I'll call the officers tasked with following up with the laundry as soon as we're done." She didn't want to interrupt the flow of information in the meeting to chase every new lead. "What else?"

"We've found no one who witnessed Karen walking out to her van," the female investigator reported. "There's only a few security cameras in the vicinity of the café and none work. Unfortunately, we've chased a lot of dead ends."

"Keep chasing." Charlotte understood the discouragement that crept in at small increments with each failure, until the negativity stalled the case. That was how they went cold. Investigators grew tired of working hard for no results. Departments pulled resources due to lack of outcomes. People's attention moved to the next crime. The next crisis.

The Presque Killer and his victims, though, hadn't left the minds of those in the community.

"Next, I'd like an update from the team working the Ginny Gerard murder." Charlotte pulled her thoughts to the present. "Any new evidence come to light?"

"No," Sergeant Monroe, from the Louisiana State Police, answered. "Nothing new from the report provided of the initial investigation. Baton Rouge police canvassed the area Ginny was last seen. No one has come forward with any information as to who she came in contact with after she left the club on Tuesday, the night she disappeared."

More disappointing news. Although she'd expect to be notified immediately if a new piece of information came to light, hope remained that something positive would be presented at the task force meeting.

"Did you review the autopsy report?" Austin leaned forward in his chair, forearms resting on the glossy table surface. Other than a smooth pad of paper and pen, nothing else was on the table nearby. Austin was the neatest person Charlotte had ever met. He served as a balance to her inherent disorderliness.

"I did," Sergeant Monroe said. "The method of killing and other evidence, such as the red rope and skin carving, point to the same killer as six years ago. I agree that the victim was killed somewhere else and then dumped in the location she was discovered. Not enough ground was disturbed to indicate a struggle. Wood slivers were found in her clothes and back. My theory is she was lying on a plank floor when she was strangled. I've checked which local stores might have sold the killer's type of nylon red rope in the past six months. No reported sales, so I'll enlarge the search area. If he purchased it online, then the possibilities are endless. I followed the cold cases closely as an officer in the Baton Rouge Police Department. The killer always seemed one step ahead of the investigation back then. He still does. I'd love nothing more than to get a jump on him and haul the guy to jail."

A nod of agreement rippled through the meeting's attendees. Ten law enforcement professionals added their skills to Charlotte and Austin's efforts. Would it be enough to stop a killer?

She asked and received updates from the rest of the investigative teams. One was assigned to visit the local neighborhoods, gathering information and proactively convincing young women to stay off the streets at night. At any moment, the killer could take another victim.

Charlotte had booked a press conference to be held soon. She'd consulted with the chief and Austin about which facts should be provided to the public and which ones needed to stay confidential. If the killer wished to play a game, Charlotte would craft one of her own. Could she taunt him to come out of hiding and make a fatal mistake? Speaking live to the media and the public was a gamble as everyone needed to be tight with what they shared. But she was running out of time and could no longer play it safe.

Minutes before the press conference was scheduled to start, Austin's cell phone rang. His FBI supervisor's name appeared on the screen. He considered letting the call go to voice mail then calling him back after the press conference. But in the years he'd worked under Supervisory Special Agent Booth, the act of ignoring a call never ended well for the agent on the receiving end.

"Walsh here." Austin stepped into an empty room that seemed to be an interview area. His reflection showed on the mirrored glass window.

"Your update last night was lacking," Booth barked. "I have a decision to make and I need to know what's happening in Presque."

Decision? That caught Austin's attention. The only decision his supervisor would make at this point was one Austin didn't want to consider. "As I indicated last night, the investigation is moving slowly but we have a strong team. There was an incident late last night at Detective Reid's house. The man known as the Presque Killer broke in and left a note. Everyone here is fully committed to catching the killer."

"I know the killer you're searching for has given a tight deadline." Booth sighed. "I'm considering sending a different agent who'll have a fresh perspective. You could be too close to these cases and it's not prudent to leave you somewhere you're not effective."

What he'd feared from the moment he landed in Louisiana. His experience with the cold cases could be twisted to be a handicap. "I've had six years of distance from the first investigations. The serial killer is active and giving us a deadline. There's no time to bring another agent up to speed."

"I've already got Kolinski studying the old and new files." Supervisor Booth mumbled directions to someone inside his office before returning to his conversation with Austin. "There's an incident in New York that requires an expert in serial killers. You're my best option."

"I can't leave." Panic rose. He loosened his tie and heat rushed inside his body. Immediately, he thought of Charlotte. No hope remained of a romantic relationship but he cared deeply about her. Another abandonment, which was how she'd view it, would stick a sword through the heart of their delicately restored partnership. "I mean, I'm asking you not to reassign me."

"You don't get to make that choice. Expect another call soon. And you better answer it."

The call ended, and Austin lowered his phone from his ear. Following orders he disagreed with became more difficult the longer he was in the FBI.

He turned on his heel to leave and spotted Charlotte standing in the open doorway. *You should have closed the door.*

Her eyes conveyed betrayal. "They're pulling you from the Presque cases?" An accusation.

Moving forward, he reached for her arm, trying to convey loyalty with his touch.

She jerked away.

"It's an option my supervisor is considering. There's a situation developing in New York State. Another potential serial killer."

"He knows there's a serial killer in Presque, right?"

Charlotte snorted. "We are in the middle of the fight of our lives, for my life and others, and the FBI wants to pull the only agent with working knowledge of the cold cases. And…who has been here, with the investigation, since I was kidnapped."

He held out his hands, palms up. "Nothing has been decided. And if Booth does order me to a different case, I won't go."

"You say that now, but when your job is on the line—" she bit her lower lip "—you'll follow orders."

His heart ached for the disappointment he'd caused when leaving before. He'd never blamed her for her hostility. Austin regretted his earlier lack of spine. He wouldn't make the same mistake twice. "I'd see this through. Your life is under threat. I'd rather be fired than abandon you."

She turned away and lifted her chin. A wall of emotional armor fell around her, as visible as if she were dressed for battle.

Was he prepared to leave his career so he could remain at Charlotte's side? He'd worked hard and dedicated many hours while advancing in the FBI. He'd studied and held knowledge not many others had.

His supervisor's call conveyed a reminder. They'd find the Presque killer, arrest him and complete the job. A new assignment would follow, chasing another criminal. His collaboration with Charlotte ended the moment their task was complete. He couldn't lull himself into believing he could find a forever happiness, not in Presque, not anywhere. As long as he worked for the FBI, and he loved his work, the possibility of a wife and family didn't exist. He chased evil into the shadows. Protecting others from experiencing the darkness, especially ones that he loved, compelled him to avoid serious relationships.

If his supervisor directed him away from the Presque cases, Austin planned to contest the command. He'd have the facts ready to support his continued assignment. At this moment, both his service in the FBI and Charlotte were important. He'd fight to stay. The victims deserved nothing less.

TEN

Charlotte stood inside the police station, taking deep, steadying breaths. A crowd of press and members of the public had gathered outside. People wanted answers. They were scared and worried. A serial killer was hunting in their midst. The questions sure to be asked echoed in her head. Why hadn't the police and FBI been able to stop him yet? Did they not care about the women murdered? How many more women needed to die before the killer was caught? Charlotte wouldn't be spared scrutiny because her own sister was a victim. She still represented and led the institution that had failed to catch a killer.

"Are you ready?" Austin looked over his typed statement before placing it inside a leather folio.

Ready for you to leave? Overhearing Austin's phone conversation with his supervisor had been a punch in the gut. Old feelings, ones she'd thought were buried, had come roaring back. Her attraction to him had been based on his good looks, kindness and competency on the job. Still was. She'd have to remember he wasn't staying, and bringing the killer to justice was her number one priority. If Austin didn't serve to help, then he was a liability. She couldn't allow herself to become emotionally entangled with him again.

"Ready as I'll ever be." She folded the piece of paper

holding her handwritten notes. The rest of the task force was gathered behind them, ready to follow her and Austin outside to face the reporters and cameras. "It's time."

As she stepped outside into the sunlight and heat, the sight of the crowd left her dizzy. She scanned the faces of those gathered. Was the Presque Killer in attendance? It was very likely, as serial killers enjoyed watching the investigation into the crimes they committed. They loved attention. This killer wanted Charlotte's every thought to be directed to him. And a press conference to discuss him and his actions was the top prize.

The department's communications staff member along with the building maintenance team set up about thirty chairs in rows in a grassy section near the parking lot. For the comfort of the press conference attendees, most of the chairs had been placed in the shade of two ancient live oaks. The presenters weren't so lucky. The podium and area for law enforcement were located on the hot cement lot under a ten-foot canopy.

Austin quickly put on his trademark special agent sunglasses, causing Charlotte to almost smile. She wore a Presque PD baseball hat to protect her eyes. Not nearly as debonair a look.

She moved to the podium and checked with the sound engineer before speaking. After welcoming those in attendance, she introduced the task force set up to nab the Presque Killer and then provided a brief update on the investigation while omitting certain facts they didn't want known to the public. Like the fact that Charlotte herself was a target. If the killer were watching, either live or on TV, she wanted him to know that he hadn't frightened her. At least not enough to stop searching for him. She was still here in Presque, hunting him. He hadn't scared her away.

Once she read off her notes, she slid over to allow Austin to speak. He provided a high-level overview of the federal resources allocated for the investigation. During his speech, a hush grew over the gathering. FBI special agents were only sent to significant crime scenes meeting their threshold for violence of the crime or the number of victims. His return proved the FBI agreed with local and state law enforcement about the seriousness of the Presque cases.

Austin took a few questions and provided concise answers.

"Detective Reid," a reporter shouted out. "Residents of Presque and the surrounding communities are scared. One woman has been killed, another gone missing. All in less than a week. The killer hinted that he wouldn't stop until he was caught. What reassurances can you give the local residents that they or their loved ones won't be next?"

Every question that came from Ronald Rheault's mouth felt like a personal attack since the first time she'd encountered him professionally almost ten years ago. She'd been a new officer, fresh out of the academy. A fumbled arrest and an escaped criminal had made her a target of Ronald's scrutiny. He wrote a scathing article about the incompetence of new hires in the police force, using Charlotte as an example. Since that article, every time she made an error or the appearance of an error, the pesky reporter was right there to cover it. In contrast, if Charlotte experienced success, like her promotion to detective or her work on larger investigations, Ronald seemed more interested in other stories.

"I understand the concerns of the community." Charlotte made eye contact with Ronald and watched him stiffen in response. "The newly formed task force is working around the clock to locate the person responsible."

Another reporter stood in preparation to ask a question but Ronald spoke before she could get a word out.

"Why should the people who are living in danger trust the same group of people who failed to find the killer before?" Ronald asked through a smug smile.

Why are you getting pleasure out of this situation? she wanted to question him right back. His attitude had been strange since the day the first murder victim was found. Charlotte had believed he loved the thrill of chasing a big story in an uneventful small town. Could it be more?

"Only Special Agent Walsh and I are from the initial investigation six years ago." She glanced over her shoulder and caught Austin's puzzled gaze. Did he have the same concerns about the overzealous reporter? "The rest of the task force was brought in for their investigative skills and fresh perspectives."

The other reporter opened her mouth to try again to ask her question, but Ronald drowned her out. "A source told me that the Presque Killer has said you, Detective Reid, is his motivation this time around." Standing about ten feet away from the podium, Ronald leaned forward slightly. "Given that your sister was murdered during his first spree, the killer could have a personal vendetta against you. Do you feel your participation in the investigation may hinder its progress? He may view your attempt to bring him to justice as a challenge, one he needs to answer with more violence."

Her knees buckled, and she clutched the podium for support. Who had leaked the killer's connection to her? Someone on the task force? One of the officers who'd answered the emergency call when her home had been broken into and they found the killer's note? Whom could she trust? Did anyone have her back?

Austin placed a hand on her shoulder and gently moved her to the side. He raised the microphone to his mouth. "Whatever information you have is pure speculation. Of course, many details of our investigation are confidential, and believing everything you hear whispered on the street is not good journalism."

"I'm only attempting to validate my information." Twirling his pencil between his fingers, Ronald glanced around at the other press conference attendees as if attempting to gather support for his assertive tactics. "Provide a comment, Detective Reid, so I don't go making up stories, as you put it yesterday."

"We have no comment about Detective Reid and any possible motivation for a serial killer." The firm tone in Austin's voice quieted the mutterings of the crowd. "Why someone tortures and murders innocent women is something I don't fully understand and I've been studying serial killers for more than eight years. A serial killer might state a motivation but what it comes down to is that the person is sick and evil. That's it. There's no excuses or victim blaming. No trying to deflect blame on anyone else. Make sure to include that in your article." He pointed a finger at Ronald. "Does anyone *else* have questions?"

Even though Charlotte wanted to clap her hands after Austin's short speech, she kept her expression and body language relaxed. Her mouth was neutral, in neither a smile nor a frown. She lowered her shoulders, which had been creeping up to her ears each time Ronald spoke.

Other reporters for local, state and national news peppered her and Austin with questions. Chief Gunther stepped forward to provide his assessment as the chief of police.

As Charlotte prepared to call the press conference to a close, an elderly woman stepped from her seat to the center aisle. "My granddaughter, Mary Gury, was the first to be found, murdered by a mystery man who nobody can seem to find. I often wondered if anyone cared about her afterward. Mary had her struggles but she was a good girl who loved her family and Jesus. I know y'all are doing y'all's best but you need to try harder." The woman gripped with both of her hands the handles of the purse positioned in front of her body. "If anyone knows anything about what happened to my Mary or those other poor girls, speak up. You can't blame the police for not doing their jobs when people are keeping their mouths shut."

"Amen," someone shouted in the back.

While the woman had been speaking, Charlotte watched Ronald. Instead of writing down the woman's moving speech, he'd already moved on, zipping up the folio that held his notebook, pen and recorder.

"I appreciate everyone's time and attention and we hope to provide another update soon." Charlotte took the paper with her notes off the podium. "The tip line is open. Anyone with information regarding the murders or kidnapping please call in." Sweat beaded on her brow, and a deep feeling of sorrow tightened her lungs, making it hard to breathe. She pictured the face of Mary Gury's grandmother. A face weathered by years of grief and unanswered questions.

She strode into the station. "I let them all down," she whispered to herself. The members of the task force were dispersing further into the building, returning to the tasks they'd abandoned to attend the press conference.

Soon, only Austin remained. "You okay?"

"No." Suppressed tears burned her eyes and throat, but she wouldn't set them free. She entered the station's kitchen and lowered herself into one of the plastic chairs that surrounded small, round, wobbly tables. With her feet placed wide, she rested her elbows on her knees, folded her hands and rested her forehead on her entwined fingers. She prayed for endurance and forgiveness.

"Hey." The scraping of chair legs across the vinyl floor announced Austin's presence. He scooted his chair closer and placed a hand on her shoulder.

They sat in silence for a minute, facing one another, until Charlotte finished speaking to God. She lifted her head to the sight of Austin's handsome face only a foot away. "I feel like I'm losing every battle. And hearing the woman whose granddaughter was the killer's first victim was a knife to the heart. I failed everyone in this town, including Ruby."

"Every person who's worked on investigations like this feels the same way at times. I do." Austin pulled his hand from her shoulder and straightened in his chair. "I struggle with the fact the killer has eluded us for so many years. And now he's resurfaced with a vengeance and put you in his crosshairs."

"I can't dwell on his threat to me." She sucked in a breath. When Austin had pulled away slightly, he'd created more distance between them. She fought to maintain her professional demeanor when all she wanted to do was be wrapped tight in his arms. "I'd give anything to have my sister with me again. Ruby was the only one who really understood me. Growing up, we only had each other. It's so hard to deal with struggles in my life without her."

Austin stayed silent for a moment. When he spoke, his voice cracked. "You're not alone. I know I'm not your sister but lean on me as I'm leaning on you. We'll get through this. We may be losing ground in our current battle but we will win the war and the killer will face justice. Have faith in God and in me."

She had faith in God. It was Austin she doubted. Would

he leave if directed to? How could he not? He was good at his job and held knowledge needed to find the bad guys. The world needed Austin, which meant she'd say goodbye to him at some point, likely soon.

When she glanced at him again through eyes blurred with tears, Austin's face drew close. His lips brushed her cheek then her mouth.

For a brief moment, her surprise caused her muscles to stiffen. But his warm touch melted her resolve. Another soft kiss reignited a longing she'd put away years ago.

He pulled away. "I'm sorry." His voice was husky.

Thank goodness they were seated in the corner of the station's kitchen, out of the view of anyone walking by the door. Their brief connection had brought back all the regret she'd felt after the last time she let her guard down and kissed him. Instead of focusing on solving the cases, her head had been filled with dreams of a future with Austin. Now she knew better. Grab a moment of happiness but don't expect more. She'd savor his kiss. Place the memory securely in the back of her heart. "When the going gets tough, we kiss."

Austin's sad smile almost cracked her resolve.

While fighting to not give in and kiss him again, she pushed up to her feet and locked away her emotions. The Presque Killer wouldn't turn himself in. She had work to do.

ELEVEN

The next morning was Sunday. The Lord's day. Even while traveling for work, Austin liked to attend church. Charlotte had invited him to accompany her to the early service at hers.

He'd barely slept. His mind had oscillated between the kiss with Charlotte and the prospect of his supervisor reassigning him.

That kiss. He knew better than to walk the path of heartbreak again. Their last kiss had ended in disaster. Charlotte blamed herself for not finding Ruby in time. And he blamed himself for letting his feelings for the detective in charge of the Presque Killer investigation cloud his vision. The personal connection between them served as a distraction, yet he struggled to keep their relationship strictly professional.

He believed God put people together for a reason. In Charlotte and Austin's case, the purpose wasn't to find love and a spouse. Instead, they made a great work team. His neatness balanced out her chaotic approach to a problem. Charlotte's broad way of observation enriched his logical point of view. She kept him balanced and grounded—and added a ray of sunshine that illuminated the darkness of their investigation.

He checked the date on his cell phone despite the countdown ticking inside his mind. Today was day three of seven. They had only four and a half more days to stop the killer. Time was running out.

Even so, he'd carve out an hour to honor God and ask Him for guidance. Time with God was never wasted.

He exited his motel room to find Charlotte waiting on the walkway. She'd traded her jeans for a blue dress and black heeled shoes. Her blond hair was twisted in a bun at the back of her head. A few strands framed her face. She looked beautiful, as always. What else did she enjoy doing other than chasing criminals? She held a deep faith in God, but when had her relationship with Him begun? He doubted she'd been brought to church by her mom, so who introduced her to the Lord? So many questions that might go unanswered.

"Good morning," he said as he approached. "You get any sleep?"

She shook her head. "Barely." A yawn escaped her lips. "I'll sleep for a year once the Presque Killer is behind bars."

He imagined once the case was over she'd turn into a maiden in a fairy tale who'd been placed under a sleeping spell. Would his kiss break the curse? *Get those crazy notions out of your head.* Especially now, when Charlotte's life was in danger. If anything, Austin had to slay the dragon hunting her.

"I'll drive." She dangled her car keys. "We're going to church and the black special-agent-mobile attracts too much attention."

"It's a regular SUV that's black." He went to her car, a silver sedan, and waited by the passenger side for her to unlock the doors.

"With tinted windows and an FBI special agent behind the steering wheel." After unlocking, she opened the door and seated herself. "You still look like a dashing secret agent but at least me and my boring car go unnoticed."

"I don't look like a dashing secret agent." Though he did like hearing she thought him dashing. His objection held an undercurrent of humor. He was more a workhorse than show pony. But her teasing created doubt. He took stock of his clothing, the same type of pants, shirt and tie he always wore. "Do I?"

Charlotte started the car, then pulled out of the hotel's lot. "I've never seen a real secret agent, so I can't say for sure." The car radio played classic country. She lowered the volume, quieting the soulful twang of Patsy Cline.

"I have. During a trip to London, I attended training with MI6. The experience was exhilarating and terrifying." His service in the army and FBI had gifted him with many exciting experiences. Some dangerous. Caleb had told him that someday Austin would find balance and start a family. In Austin's opinion, work was life. Work gave him purpose. If not for his position with the FBI, he wouldn't be with Charlotte at this moment, helping her catch a serial killer.

"I bet training with MI6 was awesome." She reached for her cup of coffee set in the cup holder while keeping the other hand on the steering wheel. "When I was little, I wanted to work for the CIA, go on undercover missions. Ruby would hide clues for me to follow. She was always such a good sport to play along with my fantasies."

"What you're doing now is just as important as a CIA mission." He watched her sip her coffee while driving, anxious she'd spill on her silky dress. But unlike Austin, she could do more than one task at a time and returned the cup to its holder without spilling even a drop of coffee.

"Maybe someday I'll live my dream and become a spy." She turned into the church's parking lot. Most of the spaces were already full as Charlotte and Austin were arriving seconds before the bell tolled to announce the start of worship. She found one at the back of the lot and parked. "But for now, I will clear my mind and cast all my cares on God."

Walking up the front steps of the church, he regarded the wide double doors, flung open to invite all inside. He entered beside Charlotte, noticing her shoulders relax. The nave of the church wasn't large. Each wood pew held parishioners.

Charlotte found an empty spot in the back. They remained standing as the pastor positioned himself before the altar. He began to speak, welcoming members and guests. The piano played the opening notes of the first hymn. Austin sang along with the familiar verses, feeling some of the gloom from his spirit begin to lift.

"God is good," Austin said along with the congregation when the pastor motioned for them to be seated.

Making opportunity for worship was a struggle when working an active case. Thankfully, Charlotte believed in the value of church. A person took breaks from work for eating and sleeping. Wasn't praying even more necessary? No one offered more protection than the Almighty God.

When the service ended, Charlotte experienced peace she hadn't felt since she'd learned the Presque Killer had killed again. Perhaps it was Austin seated close beside her. Or the pastor's words of comfort during his sermon. When she invited Austin last night, he'd surprised her by eagerly accepting. While they spent hours working together, the subject of faith rarely came up. She knew he believed in God. How could he spend a career studying the worst of humanity and not question why God allowed evil to prosper? During dark, lonely nights, she'd lie in bed and engage in a one-sided debate with God. Why had He allowed Ruby to die? What was Charlotte's purpose once the Presque Killer was caught? Would he ever be caught? And more recently, would her life end by her sister's killer if she failed to stop him?

She left the sanctuary of the church, stepping into the humidity waiting outside.

"Hello." A man wearing a shirt and tie approached. A petite woman with long blond hair kept close to his side. "Don't know if you remember me. I work as the assistant to the medical examiner in Baton Rouge. I was there the other day when you visited Dr. Connor. My wife and I are thinking of joining the church. The one we've been going to hired a new pastor who's a little too fire-and-brimstone for our tastes."

Charlotte shook hands with both the man and his wife. "I'm sorry but I don't remember your name. When I'm at the medical examiner's office, I'm singular focused."

"No worries. Robert and Vanessa Sinclair." He glanced over at Austin. "Good to see you again, Special Agent. We live in Royal, about ten miles from Presque. My wife and I are nervous about what's been going on. Have you made any progress in finding who's responsible?"

Vanessa held tightly to her husband's hand. "I won't go out by myself anymore and check in once I get to work."

"That's good," Austin remarked. "We're working hard to get this guy but for now, remain vigilant."

"If you need information from the medical examiner's office, ask for me when you call," Robert said. "Dr. Connor is busy, and I know you need answers fast. Here's my card with all my contact information."

"Thank you." She accepted the business card and slipped it into the front pocket of her purse. "Did you like the church service?" Charlotte asked despite the urge to rush back to the station. The task force was meeting again in a few hours.

"We did," Robert said with a smile. "I think we're ready to transfer our membership. My wife just found out she's expecting, so it's a good time to make a change." His smile faded. "Is that a news reporter?" He pointed to a man standing on the sidewalk, holding a camera in their direction. "He's shown up at the medical examiner's office too, looking for a statement. No one there would talk to him. The woman who works the front desk used to be a professional wrestler. The reporter didn't have a chance."

A scowl grew on Charlotte's face. Ronald Rheault. Could she not get a moment's peace from the man? Not even church saved her from the reporter's constant scrutiny. "He's everywhere these days."

"I saw the press conference yesterday at the police station," Vanessa said. "That reporter was rude and abrasive. Totally uncalled for, given the circumstances."

Ronald appeared to snap a few more photographs before blending into the crowd of parishioners leaving for their cars.

Filled with both anger and suspicion, Charlotte asked Austin to wait on the church stairs while she marched in the direction Ronald had taken. Why the interest in her? Did he believe she was hiding the key to solving the mystery of the killer or did he already know the killer's identity? "Ronald," she called out. "Stop."

He skidded to a halt about half a block away from the front steps of the church, then spun to face her. "Is that a police order?"

"A personal request." An image flashed in her head of this man overpowering a woman, taking her and killing her. Had he been the one who'd held her captive, tied to a chair in the basement of the house outside of town? Ronald was tall but thin. Was he strong enough to be the Presque Killer? "What are you doing here?"

"Following my story." He took out a voice recorder and pressed Play. "A killer is on the loose and the lead detective along with her FBI partner take time away to attend church. Don't you feel your time is better served protecting the community from the person killing local women?"

"Do you believe in God?" She took the measure of this man, who appeared to get some sort of weird pleasure from asking Charlotte passive-aggressive questions. A serial killer usually stayed under the radar for as long as possible. Attention drawn could result in suspicion and an arrest, cutting off his activities. Ronald didn't seem to have those qualms. If he was the killer, did he believe his role as a reporter gave him access to the investigators and their work without anyone questioning his motives?

"God is a construct made by people who wanted to control others." Creases appeared between his eyebrows. Ronald's gaze lifted to view over Charlotte's shoulder. "Your FBI friend appears concerned. How's the reunion going? A police detective and FBI agent make an attractive couple. Is love in the air along with murder?"

"Excuse me." Austin settled at her side. "We're needed back at the police station."

"Did you get a break in the case?" Ronald directed his voice recorder toward Austin. "Anything you'd like to share?"

"No." Charlotte swatted down the recorder like a pesky bee. "If you have any more questions, contact the police department's communication liaison."

"They're not telling the media anything." Placing the recorder into the back pocket of his jeans, Ronald frowned.

Sweat appeared on his forehead, and he wiped it away with the back of his hand.

"Good," Charlotte muttered and walked away with Austin to her car. "I need to make sure it stays that way."

"Do you think it could be him?" Austin considered the idea. A harassing news reporter wasn't abnormal. Most performed their job with professionalism. Some used aggressive tactics to chase a story. He believed Ronald Rheault fell into the latter category. Could his motivations be more sinister?

"He's a weak suspect, given my suspicion is based on bad vibes. But he's still a suspect in my book." Charlotte wore a short-sleeve dress the color of the Louisiana sky overhead. The rainstorm last night had moved on, leaving a beautiful azure-colored sky with only a handful of puffy white clouds floating across.

"What's his personal connection to you?" Austin asked, pressing her for logic instead of feelings. An investigator had to rely on both. A good investigator always backed up opinions with facts.

With her eyes focused on the road, she came to a stop at a red light. "I went to school with him. I don't know which grades. He remembers me but I don't remember him. His news stories have always been hypercritical of me. I'm not a perfect cop but I don't feel I deserve being written about as a fumbling fool."

"Has Ronald ever contacted you outside of a professional interest, like to ask you out?" A rejected romantic proposal had pushed other unstable men to violence.

"No." The light turned green, and she stepped on the accelerator. "He's too busy trying to bury me in negative news stories." She checked her rearview mirror. "There's a white truck following us."

He turned in his seat to catch a view of what shadowed them. A white truck similar to the one he'd seen speeding away on Charlotte's street. "Didn't you say there's hundreds of those kinds of trucks in the area?"

"There are. Maybe I'm being too paranoid."

"A serial killer threatened your life. There's no such thing as too paranoid." Glancing back again, he watched the truck inch closer. The male driver's face was obscured by the lowered brim of a baseball hat. "Turn here."

She turned right at the next intersection. The truck copied their change in direction.

Adrenaline surged. Was this another method of intimidation?

At the next intersection, she turned right again.

The truck continued straight. Soon, he lost sight of it.

"That was probably some guy driving to meet his buddies for breakfast." Her hands trembled slightly as they gripped the steering wheel.

"You need to stay vigilant. And if that means overreacting on occasion, then overreact." He lowered the car window for fresh air. The AC was on in the car but he needed more. A pleasant fragrance drifted off the magnolia flowers that dotted the trees alongside the road. When he left town, he wouldn't miss the heat and humidity. But he would miss the sweetness that always floated in the air—Charlotte's peony perfume mingling with the scents of ever-prevalent flowers.

When they reached the police station, he breathed a sigh of relief. At least Charlotte was fairly protected inside its walls.

"I don't trust anyone anymore, present company excluded." She turned off the car and exited.

Austin got out and closed the door. He glanced at her

over the roof of the silver sedan and hooked his thumb toward the brick building that housed the police station. "Even those you work with?"

"I don't want to suspect a member of law enforcement but how did Ronald know confidential information about the investigation?" She drummed her fingers on the hood of the car.

"There's a leak. Or Ronald could have spoken with Michael." Could an informant or killer be hiding under the cover of a badge? Discovering an investigation had a leak, someone who spoke to the media without authorization, wasn't uncommon. In this instance, one of their own was under threat. What purpose did sharing the connection the serial killer had with Charlotte serve? To cause harm? "Request that Chief Gunther place a cone of silence over the entire investigation. No more press conferences. No comments on any questions going forward."

"I don't want residents to think we're keeping things from them." All the tension that had left Charlotte's body in church was reappearing. Her back was stiff, and her face tight with worry.

"We are keeping things from them for the integrity of the investigation." He rounded the rear of the car to stand next to her. Taking her by the shoulders, he turned her so she met his gaze. "We have four more days to catch this guy. After he's locked away, you can give the press conference of a lifetime."

"Are you confident he'll be captured in time?" Fear dilated her dark pupils.

"I'm confident in you...and in me." He paused. "And most importantly in God." Failure was not an option. Four more days. If the killer continued to elude them, Charlotte could lose her life. Four more days to track a madman and take him into custody. Clues remained hidden. What had they missed during the initial investigation that kept the killer concealed? All they needed was one big break. One piece of evidence that connected the dots and revealed the killer's identity. He had faith that a big break would come. But would it come in time to save Charlotte and the other kidnapping victim?

TWELVE

The piercing ring of a cell phone startled Charlotte out of a restless sleep. She looked at the time—three o'clock. Nothing good came from a call in the middle of the night.

"Detective Reid." Her voice was husky from sleep.

"It's Chief Gunther. There's been another kidnapping. Officers are at the home of the potential victim, speaking with the family. I want you and Walsh down there now. Maybe we'll get lucky and find a witness."

While he was talking, she was slipping out of her pajama shorts and into jeans. "We'll be there right away."

Chief Gunther provided the address and some preliminary details. When she ended the call, she made another to Austin. He didn't sound nearly as groggy as she felt.

In the hotel's tiny bathroom, she washed her face and brushed her hair, pulling it up in a ponytail. Taking a moment, she stared at her reflection in the mirror. Dark circles underlined her eyes. Her skin looked sallow—possibly from the yellowish bathroom light or possibly because she hadn't gotten a decent night's sleep since the Presque killer had reemerged.

She exited her hotel room, closed the door and locked it. Austin came out of his room at the same time. They were noticeably acting in sync these days. Must be due to the two of them spending almost every waking minute together. Strange to think he'd soon be out of her life again—this time for good.

"Who's driving?" He asked. His dark hair didn't have the same sheen as normal and not every hair was in perfect order. In fact, short bangs swooped on his forehead, and he brushed them back off his face with his hand.

"You can. I want to be noticed." She walked to his black SUV parked nearby. Given the lack of faith from the community, their recognizing an FBI special agent was on scene, an active participant in the investigation, would hopefully calm doubts. If the killer was to be caught, law enforcement needed the cooperation of the community. Someone could have witnessed the kidnapping but kept quiet due to distrust. No solid tips had been received so far, even after the press conference.

They silently drove to the neighborhood where the victim was last seen. Her brain had fully awakened and was currently engaged in speculation. But until she knew the facts, she wouldn't get stuck on any one theory. This missing woman could be unrelated to the Presque Killer. People were jumpy and called the police for situations they normally wouldn't.

Austin parked behind a marked squad car. The street was dark beside the couple of streetlights that still worked and the flashing of red and blue from the light bars on top of police cars. A group of people were gathered in the front yard of a house, some wearing nightwear. The house they stood before was brightly lit from the inside. More people stood toward the back of the driveway, by a rickety garage.

Charlotte approached Officer Evans, who stood leaning with his back against his squad car. "What house was the missing person last seen in?"

He indicated the house where people had assembled. "Candace—better known as Candy—Lyon attended a party at a home owned by Rich Walker."

"He's the go-to if people want drugs," Charlotte added for Austin's benefit.

"True." Officer Evans nodded. "So it's no surprise those in attendance aren't being very chatty. We all know what kind of party Rich throws."

"When was Ms. Lyon last seen?" During these drug- and alcohol-fueled parties, people stumbled off into the night all the time, making it home or onto a friend's sofa or a neighbor's front yard.

"Her dad came over to bring her home. Ms. Lyon was attending addiction counseling and had been clean for two months." Officer Evans glanced over at the source of shouting coming from the front lawn. "Her dad learned Candy had left the party a little before midnight and no one has seen her since. She didn't return home and none of her friends know where she is. Since she fits the victim profile of the Presque Killer, her father made a call to the police."

"Is Mr. Lyon here?" She scanned the crowd, which was appearing more restless by the second.

"We convinced him to go home by telling him you and Special Agent Walsh would be over to speak with the family. It's too loud here to hear yourself think."

Two men began shoving one another. Charlotte, Austin and Officer Evans rushed over to intervene.

"Did anyone speak with Candy before she left?" Austin's voice rang over the buzzing of other conversations. "Did she say where she was going?"

"She had a drink and left." A skinny woman with short red hair pushed forward through the crowd. "Candy only came to the party to talk to her old boyfriend, Scooter. They fought and then she headed out the back door."

"Did she walk or drive here?" Charlotte ask.

"Walked." The redheaded woman pointed down the street to her right. "Candy lives with her folks and their house is only three blocks down that way."

"Where's Scooter?" Austin's rigid posture and wide-set feet warned anyone considering running. Even slightly disheveled, he looked the part of a man tasked with saving the day.

Charlotte too often forgot *not* to be attracted to him. His handsome charm frequently slipped past her defenses. While she was supposed to be one hundred percent focused on her mission here, she'd caught her gaze lingering on Austin for a second more than it should have. Dreams of romance were selfish considering similar flights of fancy had been one of the reasons the murdered women's cases had grown cold.

"That's Scooter," a different woman interjected. Charlotte's gaze landed on a tall, broad-shouldered man standing on the front porch of the house. "He's a mean one, so watch out. Don't know what Candy saw in him, except maybe a good time."

"Do you know why Candy wanted to speak with him tonight?" Charlotte inquired. Could be the former couple argued and Candy stormed off to find a quiet spot to think.

"He had some things that belonged to her and she wanted them back." The lady with the red hair offered. "Did the Presque Killer snatch Candy? Is that why y'all are here?"

"We don't want to speculate. Thanks for your help." Austin smiled at the two women before walking in the direction of the porch and Scooter.

Charlotte's intention to follow Austin was interrupted

by the sight of a white truck rumbling down the street. Her alertness sharpened when she saw Michael Duncan. The man she unofficially considered a suspect. They were still waiting for the return of his DNA test to learn if it matched the sample taken from the first victim's sweater.

The truck stopped in the street and several people wandered over to speak with Michael.

She walked over and stood a few feet from the driver's-side door. "I'd like a word." The others dispersed when they saw her badge.

"What are you doing?" Folding her arms across her chest, she worked to not appear as tense as she felt.

"I live three houses down. Don't you remember paying me a visit the other day?" His scowl highlighted the lines on his face. Michael wasn't much older than Charlotte but hard living aged a person. "Had the night off and needed another six-pack of beer." A paper bag sat on the passenger seat.

She gazed down the street and found Michael's house, dark and dreary in the shadow of night. "A young woman went missing tonight. Candy Lyon. Do you know her?"

"Sure, I know Candy. Like all us know one another in the neighborhood." Michael stared at the party house and his scowl grew. "Was she at Rich Walker's place?"

Charlotte pondered if Michael had kidnapped Candy. If he were the Presque Killer, would he come back to the scene of the crime? Some perpetrators enjoyed witnessing the chaos their actions produced. She couldn't remember seeing Michael Duncan at any of the other crime scenes.

"Did you kidnap Candy?" She decided to push him to gauge his reaction. No time for a gentle approach.

"What?" His eyes widened. "You think I took her? The girl probably went to someone's place to crash." He rubbed his scruffy jaw. "I had nothing to do with it."

The denial seemed honest, on the surface. If she scratched a little harder, would she draw blood? "Do you remember this?" She lifted her arm to bring her bracelet into view. "Ruby and I had matching ones. You stole mine."

Michael snorted a laugh. "I stole a lot of stuff back then. Don't be offended. I don't remember swiping your bracelet, but you must have gotten it back."

"I did after you were removed from the home." She inhaled through her nose, trying to detect the aromas of alcohol or smoke coming from him. Nothing but a minty scent from the gum he smacked in his mouth. A person would need to be sober to pull off the types of crimes the Presque Killer had done. "You must like the crescent moon too? What is the meaning of your neck tattoo?" For Charlotte, the symbolism of the crescent moon linked back to her mom, who'd believed the small sliver of moon in the sky meant new beginnings.

He covered the inked spot on the side of his neck with the palm of his hand. "It's something I saw on TV. Are you done with the questions? I don't enjoy walking down memory lane. My time in foster care isn't something I like dwelling on."

She recognized the flash of pain that crossed his expression at the mention of foster care. Although the families she'd stayed with had been mostly kind and loving, they weren't her mom. They weren't her real home. At least she'd had Ruby. Caring for her sister had kept her mind off the loss of their mother. Ruby had needed her, and Charlotte hadn't had time for tears.

"If you learn anything about what happened to Candy, call the police station and you'll be put in touch with me." She took a step back, questioning whether she was allowing the killer to drive away.

"Girls like Candy go missing all the time, in these parts and elsewhere." He switched the transmission from Park to Drive. "No one cares. Why waste your time, Detective? Unless you're worried you might be next."

He pulled away, driving a couple dozen feet until he turned into his driveway. His taillights taunted her.

Charlotte considered chasing after him so she could press him on what he meant by *you might be next*. When she felt someone place a hand on her shoulder, she froze. Spinning around, she saw Austin. A breath of relief left her lungs, although her heart still pounded at a supersonic rate.

"Who was that?" Austin stared down the dark road.

"Michael Duncan. He denies being at the party or that he's involved at all with Candy's disappearance." The crowd around the house had mostly dispersed, whether by the direction of the cops or due to dwindling interest. She hoped the officers had taken the names and contact information of all. "I want to bring him in for questioning. He said he was coming from the store after getting beer. It's been almost four hours since Candy left the party and anyone has seen her."

"Order another officer to bring him in." Austin waved over a patrol officer who stood by the curb. "You and I can sit down with him but we don't have enough to arrest him. We'll need his cooperation. Unless we get the DNA results back and it's a match."

"And you don't think he'll cooperate with me." Not a question. Charlotte provided instructions to the officer, giving Michael's name, address and the command to take along another officer when making the house call. "We could be dealing with someone dangerous. Be on guard and if he acts or says anything threatening, slap cuffs on him and bring him in."

* * *

Shouting caught Austin's attention. A large man marched down the road, fists clenched at his side. "Where's my daughter?" His booming voice echoed on the otherwise quiet street. "Where's Candy?"

"Mr. Lyon." Austin strode up the street to meet a man visibly in distress. "Special Agent Walsh. We understand Candy was last seen at a house on this block. We have a large presence of law enforcement questioning those who were with your daughter before she went missing."

"Are you really searching or is this all for show?" Mr. Lyon glanced around, left to right. He wore tattered jeans and a wrinkled T-shirt. His bloodshot, puffy eyes left no doubt he'd been crying. "He has her, doesn't he? The Presque Killer. She'll end up just like those other girls, murdered with no justice."

Every reminder of his failure to catch the killer felt like an arrow piercing his heart. "We don't know if Candy is truly missing. Under normal circumstances, an adult will need to be missing for longer than twenty-four hours before law enforcement gets involved. The person could have gone somewhere else and not told others."

"But this isn't a normal circumstance," Mr. Lyon spit out. "There's someone hunting young women like my daughter. Last week, she applied at the local college to become a nursing assistant. She'd stopped doing drugs and wanted to make something of her life. I don't want to imagine all that being taken away." A gut-wrenching sob punctuated his last sentence.

Witnessing the raw grief of another human being ripped away a layer of the protective wall Austin had placed around his emotions when he joined the FBI. To be a good agent, he'd learned to stay elevated above the personal feelings of those affected by the crime. He was taught to view his investigation like he was floating in a balloon, gazing down at the evidence and facts. Gaining a perspective often missed by those standing too close on the ground.

Caleb had trained Austin to use all his senses, including listening to his feelings. He had given everything to the investigation of his own daughter's murder, then dedicated his life to bringing justice to other victims of serial killers. But Austin had witnessed the toll that emotional investment had had on Caleb, especially at the end of a long career. His high level of personal dedication had drained his marriage and his health, and Austin believed it had cost Caleb his life.

Standing before a father fearing for his daughter's life, Austin felt the pull Caleb had not resisted. His connection with Charlotte already threatened to rock the steady course of his career. If he allowed himself to feel too deeply, would he ever find his way back to solid ground? Or would the internal turmoil upend him, sending him plunging into unfamiliar water?

He rested a hand on the father's shoulder. "We'll find your daughter, no matter where she is."

Mr. Lyon stumbled off in the direction of Rich Walker's house, likely having questions of his own that needed answering.

"Candy's father?" Charlotte, who'd been speaking with a party attendee, asked when she approached.

Austin nodded. "He's scared to death the Presque Killer took her." As was he.

"Does he have any idea where she may be?"

"He has no idea where she could have gone." He rubbed his eyes and yawned. The hour of sleep he'd grabbed while resting his head on the hotel room table felt inadequate. "We should call together the task force and then spread out. Once the sun comes up, a group can search this area in hopes of locating something that will point us to Candy's whereabouts."

Charlotte mirrored his yawn. She'd probably snuck in as much sleep as he had. "I'll take a look around." She removed a compact flashlight from her jacket pocket and clicked it on. A beam of light swept back and forth as she moved slowly along the street, head bent and gaze pointing to the ground.

He moved alongside her. A white folded piece of paper caught the light. After placing on gloves, he picked up the paper, already dreading what message it held. *Two.*

His optimism faded. There was no doubt Candy was a victim of the Presque Killer.

In the other direction, Michael Duncan's house had a few lights on, including the one on the front porch. Two officers stood on the porch before an open front door. Austin assumed Michael Duncan filled the doorway, although his view was partially obscured by the post supporting the porch's crooked roof.

He grabbed a flashlight from his SUV and began a search for more evidence. The Presque Killer had promised to cause turmoil and terror for a week. Seven days and then he'd take Charlotte, kill her and all his kidnapped victims. The leader of a cruel game where there'd be only one winner. The killer assumed he'd come out the victor. Then he'd slip back into anonymity without consequence. But the desire for another kill wouldn't leave. He'd want another life. More fame. His name to be whispered at gatherings and feared around the country. A serial killer did not stop until he was forced to.

But Austin would protect Charlotte from the madman even if he couldn't stay long-term.

THIRTEEN

The interview with Michael Duncan had gone as Austin expected. Michael had remained evasive, refusing to answer questions, and when he did, he'd given vague responses. His DNA results had come in as the interview ended—not a match to the sample collected off the first victim's sweater.

Austin now sat in Chief Gunther's office, having headed there from the interrogation room. Charlotte had gone to the restroom, likely needing a moment to calm her nerves after facing off against someone whose animosity bled through.

"He's not a DNA match." The chief reclined in his leather office chair, rocking slightly. "Do you believe this Michael Duncan is the Presque Killer?"

Austin considered the question he'd been asking himself since his initial interaction with the man. "We can't say definitively the DNA collected off Mary's sweater was left by the killer. That's been the theory, though. And the assumption has been that the Presque Killer worked alone but he could have had help. Now the helper has begun carrying out his own sick fantasies. There are too many loose ends to know for sure."

"Michael has been a suspect in a number of crimes but never charged. Mostly drug-related offenses." Chief Gunter straightened in his seat, then pushed up to stand. "Most of the issues we deal with around here are due to drugs, using or selling, or both. And overdoses and calls for medical attention. Having a drug problem is a far stretch to being a cold-blooded murderer."

"From what I sense after the interview, Michael is not a cold-blooded killer. He seems to be clever but not enough to get away with the Presque Killer's actions. He's proud of who he is and doesn't hide it." Michael's bluntness had rattled Charlotte more than once. "I'm worried about Charlotte. She's too close. The fact her sister was one of the murder victims makes working these cases tougher. Being a target herself while searching for a killer who's someone from her past is a strain. Do we send her out of the state until the killer is arrested?"

"I'm considering doing just that." Running his hand across his buzzed silver hair, the chief blew out a breath. "Charlotte would never agree."

"You can order her off the case." The loss of Charlotte as a partner was nothing compared to losing her permanently. But he knew this case was the most important thing in her life right now. She'd declare solving it was even more important *than* her life.

"You will do no such thing." The subject of their conversation charged into Chief Gunther's office. "You're not sending me away."

"Hear us out," the chief countered. "If you're in hiding, the killer may give up his plan and let those women go."

"Or he could kill them…and others." Hands on hips, Charlotte sent both men a piercing glare. "I can't take that chance. My life isn't any more valuable than Karen's or Candy's. Or the other women who could be next."

"While I agree with you on that, the killer is targeting you," Austin said. "You're emotionally and physically exhausted. I could see how Michael was affecting you while we questioned him."

She sank into one of the upholstered chairs in the chief's office. "I can handle Michael and any other suspects we need to question. I'm not stopping until we find him."

Austin had expected her to dig in her heels, though he'd had to try. In the end, they'd catch the killer but Charlotte would never be the same. Emotionally wrung out and possibly unable to continue in the police force due to trauma. Like Caleb had been at the end of his career in the FBI. Within a year of retirement, he'd been diagnosed with heart issues. Five years later, a heart attack stole his life.

"Charlotte, I know how committed you are to our mission. If you went into hiding for your own safety, you could trust me and the rest of the team to complete the job." Austin handed her a bottle of water that he'd taken earlier from the chief's mini-fridge.

She twisted off the top and took a drink. She appeared to consider his heartfelt plea and visibly relaxed. "I will not leave Presque while the killer I've been chasing for more than six years wanders our streets, creating mayhem. I don't care if I'm as emotionally damaged as a city after a category five hurricane. If I left now, I wouldn't be able to live with myself."

The shimmer of tears he saw in her eyes hit him hard. Austin understood passion and commitment to one's job. Charlotte had made it clear she was prepared to go to the cliff's edge to see this through. And he'd remain at her side. His job was to see the killer captured and the cases closed. More personally, he'd be a shelter for Charlotte during the storm they were combating.

"Okay." The chief stepped backward, hands up in a gesture of defeat. "But the offer remains on the table in case you change your mind."

A knock sounded on the doorframe. A state detective from the task force entered. "We received a match to the tire tracks found next to Karen's van." He placed a typed report with a color photograph on the chief's desk. "The tires are used in two different makes of medium-sized box trucks. We located the owners of matching trucks in a twenty-mile radius from town. And we found the driver of the one who'd been parked next to our victim's van. He's not who we're looking for. His name is Howard Meyer, and he drives trucks for an overnight delivery service. He stopped at the café that night with a coworker for pie and coffee, then they left ten minutes before midnight. The coworker corroborates his story. They were at their next stop a few minutes after midnight."

"There goes that lead." Austin scanned the report. Not likely he'd find a detail missed but he always verified. "The task force is meeting in ten minutes. We can cross off the box truck." Their list of leads had grown smaller instead of larger. What concerned him, besides the obvious lack of time until the killer's deadline, was how the killer's activity had increased but he continued to leave little to no evidence in his wake. Could he continue to stay that careful? Only one slipup—that was all they needed. One discarded item that helped make an ID. An oversight by the killer that they would pick up on.

The killer had gotten away with his crimes for so long he must be confident he'd never be caught. His actions supported the theory. Overconfident people made mistakes. Austin prayed the killer would make one soon.

By the time Charlotte left the police station, the sun had set and a half-moon hung low in the inky dark sky. Austin wanted to spend another hour reviewing case studies of other serial killers who'd been captured. He hoped something in those solved cases could shine light on a critical piece of the puzzle they were missing in the Presque Killer investigation.

Her eyelids were unwilling to stay up for much longer, so she'd packed up her notes and called it a day. If tonight was anything like the past four nights, she'd wake up with a start then find sleep evasive. After tossing and turning, she'd accept defeat, get out of bed to read and mull over her case notes.

The drive to the motel from the police station was thankfully brief. A pair of crime scene techs from the task force stood by the vending machine, trying to select a late-night snack. They waved to Charlotte as she walked by.

While she was grateful for the extra resources provided for the investigation, leading a task force meant dealing with administrative duties when she'd rather be out chasing the killer. But she couldn't be everywhere and do everything. Three victims, four including her, in less than a week meant multiple crime scenes needed perfect examinations. Nothing could be missed. Which was why she and Austin reviewed every report and photograph and statement. The killer wanted them drowning in police work.

She slipped the key into the lock on her room, unlocked the door and went inside. Humid, warm air struck her, and she noticed the absence of the hum of the air conditioner. After a brief check of the interior unit, she found it had been turned off. It had been on when she'd left in the morning. Why had housekeeping turned off her room's air conditioner when the temperature outside was topping eighty each day?

Pushing the button to turn it on, she eagerly waited for

fresh cool air to blow. Soon, a steady stream of cold air filled the room. She kicked off her shoes, leaving them lying in the middle of the floor. For a second, she considered setting them inside the hotel closet, then chuckled. She'd been spending too much time around Austin. His tidiness was rubbing off.

Since she hadn't had a chance to shower this morning, sleep could wait for a few minutes while she cleaned off the day's sweat and grime. Inside the bathroom, she turned on the water, anticipating standing under the spray and feeling clean again.

She'd left the bathroom door open a crack, and while she took down her hair from out of the hair tie with her back toward the door, the lights went out and bathroom door closed. Someone else must be in her room.

Panic gripped her hard and fast. She clutched the handle to the bathroom door. It turned but when she pulled on the door, it wouldn't budge. Trying again, she was left with the same result. Charlotte pounded on the door in the blackness. "Help. I'm stuck." Had she locked the door behind her when she'd entered the hotel room? She assumed so, as the action was a force of habit after years as a cop.

"Help!" She banged on the door again. Nothing. Not even budging a fraction of an inch. Now what? Her cell phone sat on the bed where she'd tossed it. The compact bathroom had no windows.

She shut off the water in the shower. A faint sound coming from outside the bathroom made her press her ear to the door. *Tick, tick, tick.* The ticking of a clock. Realization produced a shot of fear. Was the Presque Killer inside her hotel room? Had he locked her in the bathroom? For what? To taunt her or to do her harm?

"Detective Reid." A familiar digitally altered voice came from the other side of the door. "Time is slipping away."

"You never said harassing me was part of your game." Anger was slowly replacing fear, though terror still held a tight grip.

His laughter in reply nauseated her.

"Are you afraid I'm getting close? Will you keep me locked away so I can't find you?" She could taunt as well.

"I enjoy our time together, that's all," he said.

"My FBI partner will be here any moment." A bluff. Worth a shot.

"Your FBI agent is an honorable man and not one to join a woman in her hotel room at night. I believe we're safe from interruption for a while."

Unfortunately, the killer was right. "Say what you need to say, then let me out." She pounded on the door again for emphasis.

"Three more days, Detective. Midnight is approaching, then you'll have seventy-two hours until time runs out." A ringing of bells replaced the ticktock of a clock.

She imagined a brass clock with a white face topped by a pair of bells. The hands of the clock read midnight and the bells rang out an alarm. The sound ended abruptly, replaced with an equally chilling silence. She gripped the door handle and pulled with all her strength. If she could get out, she'd have a chance to catch him. The darkness enveloping her made the small bathroom feel as tight as a casket. Panic rose. She pounded on the door and yelled. Someone had to hear and come in to get her out.

Finally, she sat on the closed lid of the toilet and concentrated on taking slow, steady breaths. Not even a sliver of light shone from underneath the door, meaning the power to her room must have been cut. The killer likely had been hiding inside her room when she'd arrived. With members of the task force staying nearby, the killer had taken a risk by sneaking into her room. Doubt swirled in her mind about the integrity of the team and other members of the Presque Police Department. Had the killer evaded capture because he had insight into the investigation?

She hated doubting others like herself who'd sworn to serve and protect. Outside the bathroom, her cell phone rang. The ringing ended, likely with the call going to voice mail. Then it rang again—and again. Someone was trying to reach her. Would they give up and try again in the morning? *I don't want to be stuck in here all night.*

A pounding noise started, seemingly coming from the hotel room exterior door. She stood and struck her fists into the bathroom door. Then silence. Hope was fading she'd get out of the bathroom before sunrise.

The faraway echo of voices gave breath to optimism. She pressed her head against the bathroom door.

"Charlotte!" Austin shouted from the other side of the door. "Are you in here?"

"In the bathroom." She sagged in relief. "I've been locked in."

"I'll have the door opened soon." A thump heralded the opening of the bathroom door.

She rushed into Austin's open arms. "He was here. The Presque Killer must have been waiting in my room. I went into the bathroom to shower and he locked me in. He wanted to remind me of our dwindling time to stop him."

Austin's arms tightened around her. "You're safe. Did he hurt you?"

"No, besides giving me a fright." Resting her head on his chest, Charlotte listened to the steady beat of Austin's heart. In his embrace, she felt safe and protected. Being with him was like lying in bed on a cold morning underneath a comfy blanket, knowing the cocoon of warmth and security would dissipate as soon as she removed herself from under the covers. His was a temporary shelter. She'd be wise to remember that.

A length of red nylon rope rested on the ground. The killer must have tied it to the door handle and secured the other end to the heavy dresser set against the wall.

His hand cupped the back of her head, and he kissed her gently on the forehead. "Please reconsider leaving town. I couldn't bear it if something happened to you."

"I can't." Her words were spoken as fact, as if she'd reported her name or address. "It's my job to stop him."

"Don't let him drive the narrative. We keep pushing back. The press conference may not have flushed him out like we'd hoped but we're not giving up."

"He's messing with me." She raised her gaze to meet Austin's and almost became lost in the warmth of his brown eyes. "I won't let him win."

"But at what cost." He sighed and let his arms fall, releasing his hold.

The chill of loneliness returned. Charlotte thought of Ruby, who'd been her best friend. When Ruby had gone missing, Charlotte had found comfort in Austin's embrace. In his kiss. She'd believed Ruby would be found, the Presque Killer captured, and Charlotte's blossoming romance with Austin would bloom into love. How had she been so naive? Allowing ideas of falling in love again could not be allowed to take up space in her brain.

"At least agree to have someone posted outside your room at the hotel at all times to make sure this doesn't happen again." Austin's gaze moved around the dark room. "Is this your clock?" He pointed to a brass alarm clock placed on the table.

"No." It looked like the kind she'd imagined while trapped in the bathroom. "A gift from the Presque Killer." Her hotel room was a crime scene. Yet again, she needed to move. This time to a different motel room. "Did you see anyone lurking around outside when you arrived?"

"No one suspicious-looking." He pressed a hand to the small of her back and led her to the opened door of the room. Fluorescent light spilled in, bathing the room in an eerie, bluish glow. The power had been cut to Charlotte's room alone. "When you didn't answer my call, I became concerned."

"Lucky for me you checked in before heading off to your own room for the night." God had placed Austin in her life for a reason. A short-term gift she was grateful for.

She would call the chief and report the break in. Once again, she'd pack up a few belongings and settle someplace else for the short term. The crime scene investigator team would comb through the room, searching for anything that provided an identity of the man they hunted. A hair or fin-gerprint. Even a mark from his shoe. The most obscure thing could be the break they needed.

"Every time he does something in an attempt to gloat or intimidate or scare me, there's a chance he'll leave behind a clue. As deeply as I hate the events he orchestrates, they may be his undoing." Meaning she had to stay and keep him coming after her.

While standing outside her room to call the chief, she heard the phantom *tick, tick, tick* of the clock. The sound was only in her head. Likely the killer's intentions. She had three more days until the ticking ended and the alarm bells chimed. Her chest squeezed as the pressure to find the killer increased by the minute.

Tick, tick, tick. Each second pulled her closer into the killer's bull's-eye. But Charlotte had her sights set on him too. And she vowed to stop him before he had her in his crosshairs and took the shot.

FOURTEEN

Austin stood a dozen feet behind Charlotte. She'd wanted to visit the site where her sister had been found. After the being trapped in the bathroom by Presque Killer two nights ago and yesterday's frustration with their lack of progress on finding the killer or the two women he'd kidnapped, Charlotte had told him she was going where she felt her sister's presence. Austin wasn't letting her go anywhere alone.

He couldn't dispute her belief that the more the killer interacted with her, the more likely he'd leave behind evidence. Unfortunately, Charlotte's house and hotel room had been free of trace evidence. Austin didn't want her easily available to the killer in the rare hope of getting a piece of his identifying information.

He observed Charlotte, head bent in prayer. Little had changed here since Ruby's body had been dumped. The same thick gloom hung over the swampland trailing along the dirt road. Tall trees with limbs draped with Spanish moss gave the appearance of an old guard that kept out those who might travel into their lair.

Memories surfaced of the last time he'd visited here with Charlotte. Her scream at the sight of her lifeless sister had torn him apart. Ruby had been placed in a ditch between the road and the swampy area. He'd seen bodies of murder victims in worse shape but none had ever affected him like Ruby.

Nothing would bring Charlotte's sister back. Not even a life sentence for her murderer. Once the cases were solved, Charlotte would need to find a way back to a normal life. He allowed himself to imagine staying a part of her future. *No.* He'd never do that to someone he cared about. Not after witnessing other agents put their loved ones through lonely nights and worry-filled days. Some agents were professionals at shutting off their emotions while on the job and then flipping a switch to become a loving spouse once they came back home to their families. Austin, however, knew only how to repress his emotions. The fear of turning them back on and being washed away kept a tight rein on his feelings.

Charlotte turned around to face him and wiped her eyes. "Thanks for coming with me. I'd hoped for a vision or sign from God. I only heard the croaking of frogs."

"What if the frogs were trying to tell you something?" He took her hand and gave it a gentle squeeze. "God can work in mysterious ways."

Her fingers intertwined with his, as if holding hands with him was the most natural thing in the world. "I only studied frog language for a year in high school and don't remember a thing." She grinned. "No matter where we are or what's happening, you can always make me smile."

A tool for staying sane in the insanity of chasing serial killers. There weren't many tricks to make the work bearable. Humor definitely helped soften some of the hard blows. "You ready to go back to the station?"

"I'd like to visit the sites where we found the other victims' bodies." She spun back around to take one final look. A white cross painted with red roses marked the sacred spot. "If I follow the killer's path from start to finish, will I see something I missed before?"

"Do we have time for that?" He didn't need to check his phone to know the date. Today was Wednesday and tomorrow at midnight would mark the end of the killer's countdown. "Visiting all the crime scenes will take the rest of the morning."

"I have to. If you want to head to the station and keep reviewing the case files, I'll drop you off." She walked down the center of the dirt road, swatting away a multitude of flying insects filling the air. "May be best to split up."

"No." With a slap to the face, he ended the life of a mosquito who probably left its remains on his cheek. The short whiskers he'd allowed to grow pricked his hand. He hadn't shaved in two days, not wanting to waste precious minutes.

Charlotte reached her car, pulled out her purse and removed a tissue. With a soft touch, she wiped his stubble-covered jaw. "Southern mosquitoes are a different breed. They grow as big as seagulls and are as bloodthirsty as alligators."

"I've only had one run-in with an alligator, which thank goodness was uneventful. I'll stick with mosquitoes." The sighting had been during his first work trip to Louisiana. The creature had floated up to the shoreline near where Austin was taking a morning jog. It stared up at Austin with its reptile eyes before sinking into the murky water without making a ripple.

He took out a paper map from his bag and spread it over the hood of her car. "I'll visit each site with you." The locations where the Presque Killer's murder victims had been found were circled in red. The sites of the kidnappings were crossed with a blue *X*. Years ago, they'd sat for hours studying the map, trying to find a pattern or the home base

of the killer. The red circles bordered the town of Presque
with the two *X*'s placed inside the town limits. How did
all these different crime scenes connect to a single killer?
Or were they dealing with a partnership?

For the remainder of the morning, Austin and Charlotte
visited each murder victim's final location. They studied
the ground, the trees, the nearby buildings. Someone with
no knowledge of the murders would think the rural spots
held no significance. Even the crime scene where they'd
found the latest victim, Ginny Gerard, had been released
and no evidence remained of the woman who'd been disposed there.

By the time they returned to the station, pessimism had
taken root. Charlotte headed into the station's kitchen to
get a drink.

Austin went to the conference room and downed the remainder of the water in the stainless steel bottle he rarely
was without. They were running out of time. He stared
at the board filled with the victim's pictures. How could
someone kill five women, kidnap two, and be walking free?
Was the Presque Killer a phantom? Was he working alone?

Either no one had witnessed him with any of these
women or, if they had, the killer didn't appear out of the
ordinary enough to catch anyone's attention. Or were people
too afraid to talk? The killer could be someone who produced fear in the community. Once more, Austin examined the color image of the last murder victim's dump site.
Each murder victim had been placed beside rural roads of
gravel or dirt. A person could stop, then drop something
in the ditch before leaving without notice.

He opened the folder marked Ginny Gerard and pulled
out more photographs. He studied the ground around the
body and then the ground after she'd been removed. Those

narrow row-like marks in the dirt continued to nag the back of his mind. He took out the magnifying glass he kept in his bag. Examining the area with the markings, he grew certain the victim's fingernails had made the drag marks. But her fingernails were relatively clean in the autopsy photos. He rubbed his eyes. *You're imagining things.* Desperation produced all sorts of wild theories.

Humor yourself. He removed photographs of each of the other four victims, one at the crime scene and one taken at the autopsy. He started back at the first victim, Mary Gury. Nothing jumped out regarding her hands. She was missing a fake nail on the ring finger of her left hand in both pictures. He reviewed the others, using the magnifying glass and slowly sweeping across the photos to check for any inconsistencies.

He'd begun examining Ruby's pictures when Charlotte entered the conference room. Glancing up, he saw the redness of her eyes. His instinct was to rush to her and hold her close. A kiss on the forehead for comfort. Another on the lips to show how deeply he cared. But that was how hearts were broken. Kissing her six years ago had been a mistake. He'd given in to temptation again. His willpower to avoid kissing her once more before he boarded the flight home needed to remain iron-strong. He returned his gaze to the photograph placed before him on the table.

"What are you doing?" She moved over to stand beside him and sucked in a breath. "I'll never get used to seeing my sister like this."

"A death like Ruby's is never something you'll get used to. She should be alive. She deserved better than what was done to her." Austin held the magnifying glass to Ruby's right hand at the crime scene. Her gold bracelet, the one that matched Charlotte's, glistened under the strong lights that had been placed around the scene.

He lowered the magnifying glass, hovering over her hands, fingers and nails. One of the fingernails on her right hand appeared broken. All of Ruby's nails were short, but this one had a slightly ragged edge. Could she have broken it during a struggle with the killer? Austin had found it strange that no evidence was found under any of the victims' nails while each had been strangled. Usually, the victim would fight back in an attempt to save their life. The Presque Killer had sedated the victims with the anesthetic Propofol. But had they been incapacitated the entire time of their captivity? Serial killers in general enjoyed the feeling of power they got when killing. How could the Presque Killer feel powerful while taking away his victim's ability to struggle to stay alive?

Ruby's autopsy photo was set out beside one from the crime scene. He moved over to see if he could make out the ragged edge of her nail on the autopsy photo. Narrowing in on the nail on her right hand, he looked closely. The nail appeared smooth. He switched back and forth between the two photographs, comparing the condition of the nail. It wasn't the same.

"Take a look." He handed Charlotte the magnifying glass. "Ruby's nail is broken at the crime scene. It's hard to tell for sure since all her nails are short but it looks like it's been torn. Now, check out the same nail at the autopsy."

She switched to the other photo and leaned in. "Her nail is different. Like it's been filed smooth. Is that noted in the autopsy report?"

He found the report and set it on the table. A brief scan brought him to the section where the medical examiner gave a description of her nails and any evidence found in, under or around them. "There's nothing about a broken nail or that any part of the nail was removed for testing. No trace evidence was found in the area of her hands or nails."

His gut sounded an alarm. Had someone tampered with the body between the crime scene and the medical examiner's office?

How could she have missed it? Studying Ruby's nail under the magnifying glass, Charlotte dropped her jaw in shock. She slid the magnifying glass to hover over the autopsy photograph. Austin was right. Ruby's nail on her right hand pointer finger was smooth instead of ragged. "Do you think someone tampered with Ruby's body?"

"It's a possibility. Unless the medical examiner has a good reason for the alteration." Austin rested his back against the wall, ankles and arms crossed. "I'd expect any change to the body would be included on the autopsy report."

And it wasn't. Charlotte had memorized Ruby's autopsy report. It was the photographs she'd had trouble viewing. "I should have caught the discrepancy."

"So should I. We had these photographs six years ago and I didn't notice until now." He pushed off the wall and strode to the table. "I closely examined the other victims, including Ginny, the latest, and didn't notice any other differences."

Charlotte stumbled back, too angry with herself to speak. The alteration to Ruby's nail had been there all along, and she'd missed it. Instead of using the information to dig further and possibly find the killer, she'd let the photographs rest in a folder in an evidence box. She'd spent thousands of hours reviewing the reports and evidence of the cases over the years but avoided the photographs of Ruby's lifeless body. "Seeing her like this is so hard." Her gaze dropped to a photo of Ruby lying on the ground. Ruby's dark hair was splayed out, almost blending in with the brown earth. Charlotte touched her bracelet while glancing at the one Ruby wore in death. She wished to reach back in time to when her sister was alive, to hold her close and tell Ruby how much she loved her.

"We used to do each other's hair and nails when we were kids." Charlotte floated a finger over Ruby's hair and face. "I remember the feeling of the brush on my scalp when she brushed my hair. Ruby did not work with a gentle hand." Her laugh blended with a sob. "I should have been there for her. I failed her."

"You didn't." As before, Austin pulled her into his embrace.

Austin's arms were the only things holding her together while her world fell apart. Her emotions hit in strong waves, and she pulled away. She couldn't rely on him to be her rock. Life had taught her not to find footing on another. Swim alone if needed and reach shore on your own.

"I'll call the medical examiner. He could have a logical reason for the change to her nail." She opened the contacts on her phone, pulled up the medical examiner's office number and dialed.

After three rings, the call was answered. "Baton Rouge Medical Examiner's office. How may I help you?"

Charlotte introduced herself and asked to speak with the medical examiner.

"Dr. Connor is performing an autopsy," the woman on the other end said. "He started not long ago, which means he won't be free to return your call until the end of the day or tomorrow."

Tick, tick, tick. They didn't have time to wait. "Is there anyone else, an assistant, who I could speak with?"

"One of our assistants is with Dr. Connor now. I'd have to check to see if the other is available."

She remembered her conversation with Robert and his wife after church. He'd mentioned he'd be willing to help. "Is Robert Sinclair assisting?"

The clicking of a keyboard sounded. "No. He may be free to talk with you. I'll check."

"I have his number. I'll give him a call." She thanked the woman and disconnected.

"Dr. Connor is busy. Do you recall Robert Sinclair from church? We met him and his wife." They'd seemed like a nice couple, and were considering joining the church. She'd need to remember their names the next Sunday, when she'd run into them after the service.

"Do you think an assistant would have any idea what happened to Ruby's nail? He may not have worked there at the time of her autopsy."

"He's a start. We'll still need to speak with Dr. Connor but Robert will have insight into exam room procedures." She dialed the office number listed on his business card.

"Robert Sinclair," he answered with a distracted quality of voice.

"Mr. Sinclair, this is Detective Reid. We met at church on Sunday."

He coughed. "Excuse me. Summer cold. Let me take a drink of water." The line drew silent for about ten seconds. "Detective, yes, how may I help you?"

Keeping her statement of events as concise as possible, Charlotte explained the dissimilarity they'd discovered in Ruby's nail. "There was no reference to trimming the nail in the autopsy report and no trace evidence was found on her nails. Is there a reason someone would smooth her nail and not include it on the report?"

"I can't say for sure." The sound of his breathing punctuated the quiet after his sentence.

"Did you work in that office six years ago when Ruby Reid's autopsy was performed? If so, do you recall anything in the exam that stood out?"

"I've worked for the Baton Rouge Medical Examiner's office for eight years and assisted with hundreds of autopsies. I'm sorry, but the details of that particular one doesn't stand out." He paused again. "Normally, anything removed from the body, even pieces of fingernail for testing, would be cataloged and included in the report."

Her gut buzzed with hope. Had they finally found an obscure clue that would lead them to the killer? "When will Dr. Connor be free today?"

"He'll be working on the autopsy for hours, then elbow-deep in sending off reports and samples for testing," Robert said. "He has tomorrow off. A golf day, I think. You could try and catch him at the country club."

She had to speak with Dr. Connor today. If lives weren't in immediate danger, she could handle a day or two's wait. "Thank you for your insight. If you see Dr. Connor, please let him know I need to speak with him."

"Of course. Good day, Detective."

Detective. A title she'd recently been doubting she deserved. The killer called her detective to mock her. Soon, she'd no longer hear his digitally altered voice in her head.

"We're going to Baton Rouge." Her gaze met Austin's and held. "The answers we need are there and we need them now."

He grabbed his sunglasses and bag from off the table. "Are we taking the special-agent-mobile?"

"Why not? Put the miles on the federal government's tab." Gathering the photographs and paperwork from Ruby's autopsy, she cautiously placed everything inside the folders they'd previously been housed in. Taking one more glimpse of Ruby's pale face, she firmed her resolve. "Your death will be avenged. I promise you."

She climbed into Austin's black SUV and clipped the seat belt. A new clue pointed them to Baton Rouge. She'd follow its path no matter how many twists or turns it held.

FIFTEEN

Austin couldn't avoid taking his supervisor's call forever. He had three missed calls from his home office today. After arriving at the medical examiner's office in Baton Rouge, he checked his voice mail.

"I need to call my supervisor." He couldn't help but notice the grimace on her face at hearing the word *supervisor*. His obligation was to the FBI, first and foremost. If not for his job, he wouldn't be here. The FBI provided Austin with the means to use his skills to continue hunting killers, and therefore continuing Caleb's legacy.

"I'll go inside and let Dr. Connor's office know we aren't leaving until we speak with him." Instead of making quickly for the front door, she hesitated. "Will they reassign you when we may be closing in on the killer?"

"I'm not leaving. If my supervisor has other plans, then I'll convince him that my only job is pursuing the Presque Killer." Tomorrow at midnight was the deadline. A deadline in every sense of the term.

She rested her hand on his forearm. "Don't abandon me." With that plea, she went inside the office.

Austin had learned the hard way not to make promises in his line of work. The good guys sometimes didn't find the bad guy. He occasionally left without providing the answers people desperately needed. Promises were too often broken, even with well-meaning intentions.

He called his supervisor's direct line. "It's Austin."

"Walsh, about time I heard from you. You still avoiding my calls?"

"Of course not, sir." Not on purpose. Or at least not mostly on purpose. He'd rather avoid hearing the word of his removal from this case than argue with his superior on why he had to stay. "We have a potential break in one of the cold cases. I'm at the ME's office with Detective Reid to dig a little deeper."

"Do you think this break will point in a direction of substance?" his supervisor asked.

Austin had been asking himself that same question the entire drive to Baton Rouge with no confident answer. "We have reason to believe someone tampered with the victim's body postmortem."

"Keep tailing that for now," his supervisor said. "I sent you an email link with information about the three murdered hikers found in upstate New York. I'd like you up there—"

"I'm not leaving Louisiana." Disregarding orders could mean the end of his career or at least an end to further advancement.

"If you'd let me finish." His supervisor huffed out a breath. "Your skills are needed in New York. Be ready to head there soon."

"The Presque Killer will be behind bars before I leave." He prayed they'd get him locked away in time to save lives. "I'll read your email. Anything else, sir?"

"No, other than good luck."

When the call ended, Austin hurried into the office building. He exhaled a sigh of relief the moment the air-conditioning hit his face. He found Charlotte seated in a chair in the lobby.

She stood when she saw him enter. "Are you sticking around?"

He nodded. "Until the end." Taking her hand, he squeezed it. He'd told her the same thing before. This time, he was certain.

"Dr. Connor is still performing an autopsy. I told the receptionist we must speak with him." She glanced over at the pleasant-looking woman seated behind the front desk. "We could be here awhile."

Austin checked the time. Almost noon. The pressure of minutes ticking away caused a wave of panic. "I'll work on compiling a list of everyone who had access to Ruby's body after it was photographed at the crime scene."

"Good idea. I'm sure her body passed through a few hands to get to the medical examiner's office. I want to review her photographs again as see if anything else jumps out." Her face scrunched in apparent pain. Seeing a loved one's lifeless body, especially after murder, was difficult.

"I can do that," he offered. "If you want to make the calls about the chain of custody of Ruby's body."

"No." Charlotte extracted file folders from her bag. "My avoidance at viewing her pictures may have led to the killer remaining free. I need to do this." She asked the receptionist for a private room where they could work while they waited.

Once they were settled, Austin went back out to speak with the receptionist about getting the names of the transport team who'd brought Ruby's body from Presque to Baton Rouge. Someone had smoothed out her nail. Had it been an innocent action that wasn't recorded or something more sinister, like covering up evidence? With any luck, he'd find out soon.

* * *

While Charlotte waited for Dr. Connor, she studied every inch of Ruby's crime scene and autopsy photos. The task was gut-wrenching and heartbreaking, and unfortunately it showed no additional inconsistencies.

She checked her phone and clicked on an email from Chief Gunther. He provided a link to a news article, which she opened. Her teeth clenched as she scanned the article's headline—*Detective Reid Spends Time in Worship*. The rest of the article conveyed Charlotte took an hour away from the investigation to attend church. Two women remained missing. Perhaps praying would lead her to the killer, because her work on the murder and kidnapping cases was getting them no closer to providing answers for the victim's families. Included in the article were several pictures of her and Austin standing outside of church. She didn't need to read the author's byline to know Ronald Rheault was responsible.

Not wanting to subject herself to more of his scrutiny, she closed the article and set her cell phone in her purse. If only she had evidence that supported putting Ronald in jail. He seemed to enjoy taunting her as much as the Presque Killer did.

After another hour's wait, Charlotte and Austin were called back. Just like on all her visits prior, she walked down the sterile hallway and through the double doors that opened into the autopsy exam room.

When she entered, a staff member was rolling out a metal table through a door on the other side of the room, taking along the recently autopsied body.

"I hear you need to speak with me." Dr. Connor removed his gloves and then his reading glasses. "What is so urgent?"

Charlotte moved forward. "In reviewing the photographs

of Ruby Reid, Special Agent Walsh notice an alteration to one of her fingernails." She took out the two photos that best illustrated the difference in the nail and laid them out on the counter. "Her nail appears broken at the crime scene." Bringing Dr. Connor's attention to the autopsy photo, she indicated the nail of interest. "Do you see the difference?"

Dr. Connor returned his glasses to the bridge of his nose, then clipped on two small, round magnifying glasses, which he flipped down to cover each lens. Leaning in, he stared at one photo then the other, moving back and forth several times. Finally, he straightened and raised the magnifying glasses. "How peculiar. Did my report state a reason for the alteration? I will often clip off some of a damaged nail to send to the lab for testing."

Austin produced a copy of the autopsy report. "Nothing listed in your report and no nail sample was sent to the lab, or at least none that was documented. If the victim broke that nail while struggling with her killer, it held trace evidence."

"I agree. A broken nail on a murder victim, especially one who'd been strangled, would be of keen interest." Dr. Connor took the paperwork from Austin and read through it. "I can think of no reason her nail was trimmed other than someone tampered with it."

"Which is what we're speculating." Charlotte's pulse raced. "Who would have had access to a body—more specifically, Ruby's body—between the location she was found and when you performed your examination?"

"Well," Dr. Connor pondered. "I can't speak for the security at the crime scene. It's possible an officer or crime scene tech could have tampered with the nail after the photographs were taken. My transport team has possession of the body until it reaches my office. It is then transferred to my custody."

"Can you give me the names of the members of the transport team who handled Ruby's body?" Austin asked. "The woman at the front desk didn't have access to that information."

They needed names and they needed them now.

"Let me call in Cindy, who manages the office." He placed a call on the office phone set by his desktop computer.

Within a minute, a silver-haired woman rushed in. She powered up the computer, then placed her fingers on the keyboard. Dr. Connor asked her for the names of the transport team charged with Ruby's body. The office manager typed and clicked with efficiency. Soon, she pointed to two names on the computer screen.

Charlotte wrote them down. Neither sounded familiar. "Do these men still work here?"

"Yes," Cindy responded. "Here are their addresses." She printed out an information sheet on each. "Both are good workers."

Austin removed the printed papers from the nearby printer. "Who else had access to Ruby's body?"

Dr. Connor tapped his chin. "Well, myself, of course. No one else in the office besides my assistants have access to the bodies once they're in our custody."

She already knew one of the assistants. "We've met Robert Sinclair. Who is the other? And were both working here at the time of Ruby's murder?"

"Robert was." The office manager clicked through a few more screens to find the one she wanted. "The other assistant, Ken Murphy, started right before the murder. So yes, both those men worked here back then."

And both had access to Ruby's body. "Will you print out both these men's information?"

The office manager nodded.

"I don't like the insinuation that one of my employees tampered with a body's fingernail without reporting it to me." The lines in Dr. Connor's forehead deepened. "My assistants transport a body to and from the storage area to the exam room, prepare the body for autopsy, assist in the exam, then return the body to storage. At no time are they charged with doing any of the examination or altering a body without permission from myself."

"We're assuming whoever cleaned off her nail wanted to hide something." Charlotte glanced at the work ID photo of both assistants. She studied Ken's before looking at Robert's. There was something familiar in Robert's boylike face but she couldn't put her finger on what it was. Likely, she'd seen Robert and his wife at church before their conversation on the steps last Sunday.

She scanned Robert's information, including his address, phone number and starting date of employment. "Are any of these men here? I'd like to speak with them."

"Ken assisted in the autopsy I recently completed." Dr. Connor lowered onto a round, rotating stool. "Robert went home sick a little while ago. None of the members of the transport team are at the office."

When she'd spoken to Robert earlier, he had mentioned a summer cold.

"Let me call Ken and ask him to join us." The office manager reached for the phone.

"Wait." Charlotte held her breath while gazing at the work ID picture of Robert. A faint scar on his neck caught her attention. "Can I see the color photo on the computer?"

"Sure." Within seconds, the office manager pulled up Robert's image.

Now the scar was more visible. It was crescent-shaped, appearing like a sliver of the moon. The scar ran from his

Adam's apple up to his jawline. Where had she seen a similar scar before? Ruby had a crescent-shaped scar by her elbow. She'd gotten it falling off her tricycle when she was a toddler.

Charlotte pulled up her social media page on her phone and searched for Robert Sinclair's profile page. She studied the photographs on his page. Several included Robert and his wife, Vanessa. She zoomed in to Robert. There was the scar. While zooming back out, a glint of gold caught Charlotte's eye. She closed in on the image on Vanessa's wrist, and her heart stopped at the sight of a gold bracelet with a crescent moon charm. A match to Charlotte's.

"What is it?" Austin leaned in to view the screen on her phone.

"Look." She pointed to the bracelet on Vanessa's wrist then dangled hers. "Robert has a scar on his neck. I can't put my finger on it but I think he might be associated with the killings."

"Really?" Austin's eyes widened. "What connection does he have to you?"

"None that I know of." She pushed her brain to make a connection but nothing came. "Has Robert had any job performance issues or any behavior you'd consider odd?" Charlotte asked Dr. Connor and the office manager.

Both Dr. Connor and the office manager shook their heads in unison.

"He's a great assistant," Dr. Connor replied. "He's accurate and a good worker. It's hard to find people willing to do the work we do here. Some of the things we deal with are not for the faint of heart."

"Dealing with the dead is not for everyone," Austin agreed.

Viewing loss of life never got easier. And seeing the

violence people were capable of often left her questioning God and humanity.

"We need to get back to Presque." Charlotte stuffed the papers they'd received from the office manager into her bag. "Thank you both for all your help." She hustled out of the exam room with Austin at her heels.

"What are you thinking?" he asked once they exited the building. He reached for his sunglasses and put them on. The sunlight reflected off the glass front of the building.

"Robert is involved, either directly or working with the killer. I just can't put the pieces together as to why?" She came to a halt, racking her mind for anything that made sense. Why would a nice man with a wife and steady job tamper with a murder victim's body? Why did his wife have an identical bracelet to Charlotte? When Charlotte and Ruby received them as gifts from their mom, about twenty-five years ago, the bracelets had been child-sized. Charlotte had taken both to the jeweler to get them resized to fit their adult wrists. But were those bracelets sold in a size suitable for a woman? Was Vanessa Sinclair owning the same bracelet as Charlotte a coincidence?

And the scar on his neck—so similar to the carvings on the victims' arms. If he hadn't had access to Ruby's body at the medical examiner's office, she might not have paid any attention.

"I think Robert Sinclair may be the Presque Killer." Speaking the words caused her lips to tingle. They might have a real suspect after all these years. But an arrest needed evidence. All they had now was circumstantial. Regardless, they could get him off the streets for a short while. "Let's go talk to him. We can bring him into the station for questioning."

Austin gazed down at her through his dark sunglasses.

"If Robert isn't involved, we could be wasting hours focused on the wrong person."

"I know." Doubt circled in her head. "We find him, talk to him, and see how he reacts. You've spent time with serial killers. Would you recognize if Robert is one?"

He combed his fingers through his hair. "Let's go to his house and find out."

Charlotte climbed up into the SUV. She took out her wallet from her bag and found the old photograph of herself and Ruby. They were standing hand in hand on the shore of the Gulf of Mexico. Her mom had taken the girls to Panama City Beach for a long weekend. That trip had gifted Charlotte with the best memories of her family before her mom was taken away.

She narrowed her gaze to the scar on Ruby's arm. Her killer had cut a similar shape into her other arm. A memory stirred in her brain, like the rumbling of a far-off thunderstorm. It grew louder but she couldn't make out what the voice in her head was trying to say. "Ruby's scar." Holding the photo, she touched her fingertip to Ruby's bare arm. "I remember," she whispered. Ruby holding up her arm to compare her scar to someone else's. Could it be? "Before we visit Robert's house, we need to stop at my place."

Austin glanced at her with a questioning expression.

The pieces of the puzzle were moving closer. A few had clicked together. Now she needed to find the box of old photos she'd kept safe all through her youth in foster care. Inside it could be the key to solving the mystery and catching a killer.

SIXTEEN

A man sat on the front porch of Charlotte's home, and the unexpected sight of him sent her pulse racing.

"That's Mr. Lyon. Candy's father." Austin parked the SUV next to the curb in front of her house.

"What is he doing here? I'm not even staying at my house." The sight of him, tired and ragged-looking, answered her question. The father of a kidnapping victim wanted to know the location of his little girl. Was she safe? Still alive? What were they doing to find her and bring her home?

"Mr. Lyon," she said, exiting the SUV.

The tall man remained seated on her front porch steps. Finally, he pushed to his feet at Charlotte's approach. "Have you found Candy?"

Her heart ached at the anguish in his eyes. "We haven't yet, but we will. The task force is working around the clock."

"Candy is a gentle girl who never hurt no one." Mr. Lyon's voice cracked with grief. "Who would take an innocent girl? I need her back to me, safe, you hear? Bring her back."

"That's what we're working to do." Austin set a hand on one of the man's broad shoulders and squeezed. "Please go home and pray. An entire team is devoted to finding your daughter and bringing her home."

Tears filled Mr. Lyon's eyes. "I've been praying but I'll

pray some more." He moved to the sidewalk then stopped. "People say the police don't care about these girls because they had trouble with drugs and drinking. Do you care about my Candy?"

"I do care, deeply." Charlotte wiped away her own tears. "We'll find your daughter and return her to you." The pressure continued to mount. She remembered the feeling of helplessness when Ruby went missing. No amount of platitudes made that horror go away.

Mr. Lyon nodded a wordless acknowledgment and shuffled away down the sidewalk.

She hurried to the back door, then tore down the crime scene tape crisscrossing the entryway. The yellow plastic ribbon floated to the ground. She unlocked the door and went inside.

"What do you need here?" Austin glanced around the kitchen as if anticipating the killer would jump out from a dark corner.

During the ride home, she didn't give voice to her memories. They were so faded that she questioned whether she'd summoned a false recollection due to desperation. And she was desperate. Two frightened women were being held by the Presque Killer. If the killer weren't stopped by tomorrow at midnight, those women would die. And so would she.

"There's a box of old photographs I need to look through." She made for the stairs and bounded up two at a time.

"Does this have anything to do with Robert Sinclair?" Austin questioned from behind. He followed her up the stairs and into her office. "What are you looking for?"

She opened the closet door in the spare bedroom. "Can you get that down?" Pointing to a shoebox on the top shelf, she thanked God she'd kept all the photos from her youth.

The ones with her mom were precious, and more than a few times the box had gone missing at a foster home.

Austin brought the box down and placed it in her out-stretched hands.

She set it on the bed and lifted the lid with shaking hands. "When I saw the scar on Robert's neck, it shook loose a memory of my sister comparing the scar on her arm to another's similarly shaped scar. I see it in my mind's eye… Ruby holding up her arm and giggling that they matched."

"Do you think you knew Robert when you were children?" Austin watched Charlotte dump stacks of old color photographs on the bedspread. Most were partially faded. A few were spotted with water stains.

She examined every picture, looking for a boy who could be a young Robert. Most of her memories of her early years with her mom had been placed in a vault and locked away. Thinking of Mom and their chaotic lives together brought anxiety. Charlotte loved her mom, or at least the version of her she'd constructed in her mind. But she'd been afraid. Each move to a new house with a new man upended Charlotte and Ruby's lives.

She'd been eight years old when her mom was arrested and she and Ruby went into foster care. Charlotte hadn't decided which had been more traumatic—the years before the arrest or the ones after.

"My mom had a new boyfriend for what seemed like every month." She fanned through a stack of her grade school pictures. Her blond hair growing longer and wilder with every passing year. "I think she had a boyfriend with a kid. A son. They lived with us for a while." She strained her memory to fit the scattered mental images flashing in her brain. "The boyfriend was a real jerk, like most of Mom's boyfriends. But his son, I think he had a scar on his neck. He said his dad had cut him with a broken beer bottle."

Her search through the pictures intensified. It had to be in here. The recollection of standing in front of a rusty Chrysler remained too strong for it to be false.

"Is this what you're looking for?" Austin held the photo she'd been searching for.

She snatched it from his grip and held it close. Her gaze scanned over Mom, the mean boyfriend, Ruby, Charlotte and a boy about Charlotte's age. Bobby. That had been his name. She looked closely at the boy's neck, and her breath caught. There was the scar, identical to the one on Robert Sinclair. She matched it to the printout of his work ID picture. "It's him. Here's the connection." To her and Ruby.

"What do you remember about him?" Austin stood.

With the floodgates of the recesses of her mind opened, the memories rushed back. She scrutinized the picture again, noting the uneasy look on each of the children's faces. "Bobby and his dad lived with us shortly before my mom was arrested. I think his dad may have convinced her to go along with some illegal way to make a quick buck and she took the fall. Ruby and I were scared whenever her boyfriend was around, and we usually hid in our bedroom, especially when he'd been drinking. If I remember correctly, Bobby would ask to come in and stay with us, most of the time falling asleep in our room."

"What's Robert's reason for targeting you? Not that a serial killer's actions are logical but the Presque Killer has picked you. He plans to kill you. Every one of the murder victims had your body type and hair color, except for Ruby." Austin halted his pacing to stare down at Charlotte and the photo still held tightly in her hand. "He's obsessed with you."

"I haven't seen him since I was a little girl." She waved the picture. "Perhaps I've run into him at the medical examiner's office but I didn't make the connection and he never said anything. Even Sunday at church, he acted friendly but not familiar."

"We need to bring him in for questioning." Austin moved toward the doorway.

"He went home sick." Leaving the photographs spread across the bed other than the one that shifted the course of their investigation, Charlotte turned off the light to the bedroom. Could she finally be ready to take down the killer?

Austin stopped before a neatly kept rancher house. A row of bushes lined the front of the property, creating a boundary between the sidewalk and front yard. The Sinclair home appeared to be the residence of a happy, middle-class family. One car sat in the driveway. He touched his gun, which was secured in a holster at his hip.

Charlotte did the same. "Ready?" Her chest rose and lowered with large inhales and exhales.

His nerves hummed as well. A dog barked inside a neighboring house. They'd considered calling in backup and wearing bulletproof vests but decided against it. If Robert were the Presque Killer, he wouldn't be dangerous until cornered. And they might have already tipped him off that he was the killer they hunted.

The Presque Killer held two women. Somewhere. Austin was operating on the assumption they were alive. He held hope they'd be rescued before the killer followed through on his threat.

Charlotte knocked on the door then stepped back.

Within a minute, Vanessa answered. She wore athletic

shorts and a blue concert T-shirt. "Hello, Detective Reid. How can I help you?"

"Is your husband home?" Charlotte asked in a calm voice.

"Robert, no. He's at work." Vanessa glanced at her watch. "I guess he's just getting off. He was planning to get together with some of his coworkers for drinks after work, so he won't be home until late. Probably not until after I leave for work."

That caught Austin's attention. He'd theorized the killer either lived alone or shared a house with someone who worked overnight, allowing him to engage in his crimes without anyone noticing he was gone.

"Can we have his cell phone number? I need to speak with him about a case." Charlotte took out her cell phone, ready to enter his number in her contacts.

"Is this about the Presque Killer?" Vanessa gasped. "Robert said he assisted Dr. Connor with the autopsies. I don't know how he does it. I'm a nurse so sick people and death are part of my job but I couldn't handle examining a dead body."

She has no idea what her husband is capable of. Austin wasn't surprised. Psychopaths often were good at appearing normal. What better cover than a happily married, churchgoing man?

Vanessa rattled off Robert's number, which Charlotte entered into her phone.

"I'll see if I can reach him." Charlotte slipped her phone into the back pocket of her jeans. "You said you work nights at the hospital? How long have you been working those hours?"

"Since I started there about three years ago. I find it's quieter at night than the day shifts. When I met Robert and we got married last year, he was fine with me continuing to work overnights." An easy smile warmed her face. "He's good like that. Very supportive. I have to admit, though, since I got pregnant, it's grown harder to stay awake. It doesn't help I'm picking up extra shifts to save money for when the baby comes."

A baby on the way. Could that have been a stressor that tripped Robert into killing again?

"Congratulations," Austin offered. Though he feared for Vanessa's future if her husband was discovered to be a serial killer. "Hope you have a pleasant rest of your day."

Once the door closed, Austin glanced at Charlotte. More pieces fitting together. "We need to find Robert Sinclair. I don't believe for a second he's throwing back a beer with his work pals."

"Neither do I."

They returned to Austin's SUV, and he drove straight to the station. This update to the police chief should be given in person. An all-out manhunt for Robert Sinclair would commence. With good police work, he'd be found. If they could convince him to give up the location of the kidnapping victims, the community could put this nightmare behind them.

But first, they had to locate Robert. And Austin knew from experience that men like Robert, smart and cunning, were experts at remaining hidden in the shadows and were dangerous when cornered.

SEVENTEEN

We need more time. A BOLO had been issued for Robert Sinclair, who'd disappeared like a bird in flight. Austin had lived through this before—a suspect going underground after being tipped off to the interest of law enforcement. He assumed Charlotte's phone call with Robert yesterday, asking about Ruby's nail, had been the catalyst for him going into hiding. Neither of them had suspected Robert at the time.

Now he was confident that they'd determined the identity of the Presque Killer. But if Robert wasn't found before midnight tonight, Charlotte and the other women he'd kidnapped might die.

Austin had begged Charlotte this morning to go into hiding for the duration of the manhunt, but true to her stubborn nature, she'd refused. So they'd spent a long night at the station along with some of the other members of the task force, taking calls and trying to track down Robert Sinclair's location.

He'd searched for properties held by Robert and his family. Nothing besides their places of residences. Robert's home was being watched. A warrant had been issued to search the house and property. Austin and Charlotte would be heading over shortly to assist in conducting the search.

Austin stood in the conference room, staring at the pictures of the kidnapping victims pinned to the board.

"Penny for your thoughts." Charlotte approached. She placed a cup of coffee in his hand.

The rich aroma steaming from the cup hinted at the caffeine hit to come. His exhaustion was bone-deep. He recognized the same drawn look on Charlotte's face. Austin vowed to get her through until tomorrow morning alive. Then, once Robert was locked up and the kidnapping victims were safe, they'd sleep for days.

He sipped his coffee with his focus glued to the board. "I want to believe Karen and Candy are still alive."

"My gut tells me they are," Charlotte said beside him. "I think he'll want me there to watch him murder them. Some sort of performance to punish me."

"For what, though? You were both children when he lived at your home." Austin hoped to be able to interrogate Robert soon. He might not offer many answers, at least at first, but in general, serial killers loved talking about themselves and spilled their life story.

"I still don't remember much about that time in my life but living with us must have made an impression on Robert." Charlotte touched the picture of Ruby and sniffled. "What did I do that made him hate me so much?"

"You did nothing. Could be an obsession or a twisted love." Austin turned as Chief Gunther entered the room.

"We have the warrant," the chief said. "You two ready to lead the search of the Sinclair house?"

Austin left the station along with a dozen other law enforcement personnel, with the sick feeling they were wasting time. Although searching Robert's home had to be done, Austin didn't believe he'd keep anything incriminating there. To hold hostages, the killer needed a private, out-of-the-way place. A building no one knew about other than himself. Somewhere close to Presque. A headquarters, so to speak. Once they discovered that location, they'd find him.

During the drive back to the station, Austin tamped down his disappointment. No evidence tying Robert to the murders had been found at the Sinclair home. Now the game was on. Robert knew without a doubt they hunted him while he hunted Charlotte.

Charlotte rode in the passenger seat, gazing out the window. "We have twelve more hours."

He glanced at the clock on the dash. "Robert is close, likely watching us search for him. We'll catch him soon." He approached the city park and was surprised by the number of people milling around.

"The city's jazz festival starts today." She pointed to the banner hung underneath the sign marking the entrance to the sprawling park. "Let's stop. I need to walk around and clear my head."

Once he found a parking spot, they exited the SUV and strolled in the direction of music.

"I need to remind myself why I do this job." She turned her head to take in the people filling the area. Despite the threat of a serial killer in their midst, the residents of Presque had decided to go forward with the town's annual music festival. It pulled in attendees from across the state and beyond.

"People shouldn't have to live in fear." But he could see it in some of the eyes of those he passed. Parents held tight to their children's hands. Women kept in groups. The presence of Presque Police Department and Kingston Parish officers couldn't be missed.

Austin wondered how he'd feel if he came to the city festival on a day in the future, when a dark cloud didn't hang over the event. The city put on a good show. Jazz music filled the air as well as laughter. The aromas drifting from a BBQ food truck made his stomach growl with hunger, reminding him that coffee was not food.

He longed to be part of a community. He hadn't felt a real sense of belonging to a town since his childhood. His army days then career in the FBI meant a life on the move. His work was important. He stopped killers and saved lives. But at what personal cost? There'd been moments when he considered leaving the FBI to pursue a different cause. He could find another line of work that offered a better balance and allowed him a normal life. But then he remembered Caleb and the vow he'd made to his mentor. If Caleb could see Austin struggling against the pull of falling in love, would he make the same request as he had before he died? Had Caleb known the choices Austin made to continue hunting serial killers, what advice would he offer now?

What if he came back to Presque next year to take Charlotte to the jazz festival? He'd hold her hand as they snuggled on a blanket, listening to a band play songs reminiscent of the past. Could he handle sneaking in moments of a normal life? In his line of work, daydreaming could get someone killed. His attention had to remain fixed on the target, not on his beautiful partner, who'd breathed life back into fantasies of love and home. A romanticized normal existence that reality had shattered.

The shouting of a name caught Charlotte's attention.

"Lisa Ann! Lisa Ann!"

Charlotte swung toward the direction of the voice. The jazz festival was in full swing, and packs of attendees sat on lawn chairs and blankets on the grassy area by the stage.

Lining the perimeter of the park, food trucks churned out all sorts of delicious eats. But she blocked out everything else except the noise of a name being shouted through the crowd.

"Lisa Ann!" A young woman wearing white shorts and a pink tank top spun around, frantically scanning her surroundings.

Austin had stepped away to make a phone call to the FBI. The feds were sending additional resources to Presque. In addition, computer techs back East were combing databases and records for any clues on where Robert might be hiding.

Charlotte approached the frantic woman and showed her badge. "Detective Reid with the Presque Police Department. Is something wrong?"

The woman's eyes glistened with tears. "My friend Lisa Ann went to use the bathroom thirty minutes ago, and I can't find her."

Glancing to the side, Charlotte watched the flow of people going in and out of the restroom building. "Have you called her?"

"About twenty times." The woman choked back a sob. "I shouldn't have let her go alone, not with women being snatched by a serial killer. We shouldn't have come."

Charlotte set her hand on the woman's shoulder. "Take a deep breath. Let's try to locate her first before we panic. What's your friends full name? Give me a description of what she looks like and what she was wearing."

A few minutes later, Charlotte put a call over the police radio, asking officers to be on the lookout for Lisa Ann Benton, age twenty-four, approximately five feet six inches and weighing 120 pounds. She provided hair color, clothing and area last known to be at.

She took down the friend's phone number and name, praying they'd find Lisa Ann. Perhaps she'd found another group of friends to hang with for a while, or a food truck had grabbed her interest and she sat at a picnic table enjoying a paper tray full of BBQ. But what were the odds Lisa Ann was too transfixed on food to answer her friend's calls?

An hour later, Charlotte received a call on her police radio. She and Austin had spent the time patrolling the park in a desperate search for a woman fitting Lisa Ann's description. They hurried to where the officer had radioed from.

"I found a cell phone lying here on the ground." The officer directed their view to a cell phone with a pink case resting facedown on the grass. This space was set back from the main part of the jazz festival. A wooded section created a buffer between the park and an industrial area.

Austin put on gloves and turned the phone face up. He touched the screen and a photograph of the woman they'd been searching for appeared.

Charlotte's gaze concentrated on the space filled with trees and brush. She took measured steps, scanning for a footprint or anything else that might have dropped. About ten feet into the woods, she halted at a flash of light on metal. She bent over to find a silver ring partially buried under dead palm fronds. "Over here," she yelled.

The ring was identified as Lisa Ann's. Within minutes, the jazz music quieted and officers began questioning those at the park. With so many people around, someone had to have seen Lisa Ann escorted into the woods by a man.

"We have a witness." Austin ended a call. "A man with his daughter was over by the playground when he saw a woman matching Lisa Ann's description being held by the elbow by a man wearing a baseball cap and sunglasses. The witness commented that he thought they were a couple taking a break from the festival."

"He has her." Her stomach churned. The time on her cell phone glowed 4:00 p.m. "I'm next."

"No, you're not." Austin gripped her shoulders and stared straight into her eyes. "We're going to find him and the women he's captured."

Bile rose in her throat. She'd known all along the possibility of death hovered over her like an executioner's blade. Would her body be dumped in a mucky ditch like Ruby's had? Would she be found before animals got to her? She commanded herself to regain calm. She wasn't giving up. On the contrary, she planned to fight with everything she had.

Charlotte called all available members of law enforcement to the quickly established command center by the empty jazz festival stage. She directed teams to fan out and search the entire park and forest area.

Robert had likely parked his car by the industrial park then drove off with his prey. *Where have you taken them?* If he planned to come back for Charlotte, he couldn't have gone far.

"I want to take another look around the Sinclair property," she said to Austin. "Maybe we missed something." It was a long shot. His home and grounds had already been fully searched. But she wanted to walk through again. He was killing because of a sick connection to her. She might find a clue the others had missed.

"Let's go, then." Austin shot off a text while he walked along her side to the SUV. "So far, the FBI techs can't find any other property tied to Robert Sinclair or his family."

"He's hiding somewhere." She visualized the hundreds of acres of bayou surrounding Presque and nearby communities. An old fishing shack likely wouldn't have a property deed.

When she arrived at the Sinclair house, a pair of officers greeted them. After showing their credentials, she and Austin entered the house. The silence was unnerving. Vanessa had been escorted off the property and taken to her parents' house. She denied her husband was the Presque Killer, and without solid evidence, Charlotte wasn't in a position to convince her otherwise. Robert needed to be found first. A prosecutor wouldn't charge a person with the evidence she and Austin had pulled together so far.

But DNA didn't lie. Earlier, his toothbrush and hairbrush had been collected and taken to the lab for testing. A match wouldn't lead them to Robert's hideout. And they had to stop him by the end of the day. Only eight more hours.

Austin stood outside under a tall live oak that during the daytime provided shade to the Sinclair house. Now dusk fell, along with an evil darkness. He'd combed through every inch of Robert Sinclair's house and grounds and found nothing that hinted he wasn't an ordinary man living a boring life.

After studying the time line of Robert's life, Austin concluded Robert's childhood had been filled with abuse. He'd attended college and landed a job as a mortuary assistant before working at the medical examiner's office. Robert didn't seem to mind death. Actually, he'd made it his life's work. Austin calculated that Robert began dating Vanessa shortly after killing Ruby. Which explained the break. He'd tried to live a normal life. Something must have happened to trigger him back into killing, and escalating his activity. Could be the announcement of Vanessa's pregnancy. Or his path recently crossed with Charlotte. Perhaps he and

Vanessa had gone to Charlotte's church before last Sunday. Likely a combination of factors.

Charlotte approached from the direction of the house, ending a call. "Robert has vanished off the face of the earth. No sign of his car. No one has seen him since work earlier today when he left. He didn't come home." She blew out a long breath. "He's going to kill those girls if we don't stop him soon."

He checked the time. Only five more hours until midnight. They walked the property again. A small toolshed didn't provide any enlightenment. Vanessa hadn't offered any suggestions on where her husband could be. She'd closed up and hired a lawyer, who wouldn't let them near her for further questioning.

Austin tightened his hands into fists. He wouldn't allow anyone to stand in their way of finding Robert.

Tick, tick, tick. The sound in her head grew louder by the second. Charlotte knew what she had to do. They'd exhausted all other efforts. "I have a plan."

As they stood by the SUV at the front of the house, Austin's gaze snapped to focus on Charlotte. "Good, because I've run into a brick wall. What is it?"

The chorus of croaking bullfrogs seemed to keep time with her rapidly beating heart. "Robert wants me. I'm his ultimate prize. My death will satisfy his need to kill."

"I don't like where this is going." Austin scowled.

She held up her hands. "I give him what he wants."

"No," Austin barked. "We aren't sacrificing you."

"I don't plan on being killed." Though there was always the possibility. She wouldn't think about that right now. Fear of the unknown wouldn't stop her. "I'll be the bait you use to catch him."

His scowl deepened, as did the furrow lines between his eyebrows. "And what if we lose you? I'm not offering you up on the hopes he doesn't get away. Like he's had every other time, need I remind you."

The Presque Killer was smart. He'd evaded them for more than six years. "He's never taken a victim who's ready for him. I'll be ready. I will make it out alive with the women he's holding."

"No." Austin waved his hands in the air like a football referee calling a missed catch. "We're closing in on him, Charlotte."

"There's no more time." She stepped toward him, putting only inches between them. "This is the only way."

He turned his head to look away. "I can't take the chance I'll lose you." His voice cracked.

"You've sent in people undercover before," she pleaded her case. Though she'd go forward with her plan alone if necessary.

Austin brushed his knuckles across her cheek, then held strands of her lose hair in between his fingertips. "You aren't just anyone. Not to me. I trust you're capable but I'm afraid Robert Sinclair is too large a risk to put your life in his hands."

Her heart raced at Austin's touch. As deeply as she valued his concern, Charlotte refused to back down. Using her as bait was likely the only way to get to him before he killed again.

Finally, Austin broke the stalemate. "Okay," he huffed. "I'll agree, but only if you wear a GPS tracker. Two even just in case. I have some back at the police station. You wear them and we'll track your movements the entire time. We'll be able to see where he's taking you then send in a rescue team."

"We make a dynamic duo." For the first time in a week,

hope bubbled. She glanced around the dark front yard. "Do you think he's watching us?" she whispered.

"Possibly." He kept his gaze fixed on Charlotte. "You can change your mind at any time."

"I won't." Her resolution firmed to see this until the end, with Robert in handcuffs. Time to play offense. "We're going to take him down." She grinned. "I will win his game and make sure he never hurts another innocent person again."

He held open the passenger-side door of the SUV for Charlotte to climb in. "My money is on you, Reid. Always has been. Always will be."

EIGHTEEN

"Are you sure?" Austin pressed a nickel-sized disk into the insole of Charlotte's sneaker. "There's no shame in backing out."

If she decided to pull the plug and abort the mission, Charlotte would live with the repercussions for the rest of her life. That was if they were able to catch the Presque Killer before he found, captured and murdered her.

"I'm sure." Her stomach fluttered with nerves. She wasn't concerned for her safety as much as she feared failing to lead the rescue team to the kidnapped women. It was all or nothing. Tonight had to be Robert's last hours as a free man.

Austin then handed the shoe to Charlotte. "Okay, then, everyone needs to follow the plan and make sure the operation goes perfectly." He faced a room filled with SWAT team officers who'd been called in for the important job of capturing Robert Sinclair and rescuing the women he was holding captive. "Detective Reid is wearing three GPS trackers. One in her coat pocket, one sewn inside the front pocket of her jeans, and the final one hidden inside her shoe. Her movements will be tracked. It's imperative that we don't give away our surveillance. Robert must lead us to his hideout. Three women are still missing and their families are counting on us to bring them home."

A murmur of voices filled the room before quieting.

"This is what we've been working for. We will bring the Presque Killer to justice." Charlotte slipped her hand into the pocket of her jacket and felt the bump of the GPS tracker. It was no bigger than a nickel, but Austin was confident that the GPS system inside was one of the most sophisticated available. Still, technology failed. And just because they hid three GPS tracking devices on her didn't mean Robert wouldn't find them or have a way to disable the signal.

She needed to have faith—in God, in Austin, and in the men and women assembled here, ready to risk their lives to catch a killer.

"Let's go." Austin dismissed the team to prepare. He turned to face Charlotte, and his eyes held a deep well of emotion. "I have your back." If he could, he'd hide her away someplace safe until the killer was found. But letting others be placed at risk while she stayed protected wasn't in Charlotte's nature, so he'd do anything necessary to ensure she came out of the mission unharmed. "The entire team has your back. He won't hurt you."

His words sounded reassuring to her ears but her head knew there were no guarantees during an undercover mission. Too many factors that quickly could spin out of control. *Don't think about that now.* Instead, she imagined Robert being hauled away in handcuffs.

She grabbed her bag and headed toward the door. Time to get to work.

Austin followed her out into the humid night air. "I'll see you soon." He paused as she continued walking to her car.

Before she could grab the door handle, he rushed up and pulled her into his arms. "Be safe," he whispered with his lips pressed to her ear. "God be with you."

"Until we're together again." Her fear calmed. God would be with her. He'd be right beside her every step of the way. And Austin wouldn't be far either. Her heart swelled with love for the man she'd tried so hard not to fall for again.

The next part of their conversation had been preplanned. Staged for the sake of Robert, who could be watching at this moment.

"Are you sure you should go back to the Sinclair house?" Austin asked. "If you wait for about thirty minutes, I'll go with you."

"I can't wait." She added urgency to her voice. "Two officers are still there to guard the property. I'll make sure to stay close by. I just need to walk through the house one more time. I feel I missed something." Charlotte got into her car and started the engine. After waving to Austin, who stood like a statue underneath the yellow glow of a parking lot light, she exited the lot.

Soon, she'd be back under the Presque Killer's control. Only this time, she was ready for him.

At the Sinclair house, she greeted the two officers who'd been assigned to stand guard over the home of a suspected serial killer. The officers had been let in on the plan, so they faded into the interior of the house while Charlotte headed toward the backyard. She turned on her flashlight and swept its beam over the grass. Trekking across the yard, she made her way to the storage shed. She was searching for something, desperate to find the one clue that would take her to the killer. Or at least that was what she wanted Robert to believe. She had no doubt he was close by, observing her. Creeping closer.

Her hand connected with the metal handle of the shed door at the same time she felt a familiar prick at the back of her neck. She cried out, partially for performance and partially due to real panic.

"I underestimated you, Detective." Robert's real voice hummed. "You figured me out. It's going to break Vanessa's heart that I have to disappear after tonight."

Charlotte tried to speak but her mouth felt dry and tasted of metal. "No," was all she managed to say.

"Don't worry. It will all be over soon." The sound of his words grew distant.

She blinked in a futile attempt to stay conscious. How could she see where he was taking her? Her foggy mind recalled the GPS trackers. "Austin." The last thought to cross her mind was the FBI special agent she'd grown to love, who was charged with saving her.

"They're on the move." Austin sat in the passenger seat with his laptop open, his eyes fixed on a blue dot moving slowly on the screen. A group of three vehicles was lined up on a street a block away from the Sinclair house. They were monitoring Charlotte from a distance. The last thing they wanted to do was spook Robert. He held three other women besides Charlotte, and Austin believed they were all still alive.

The tracker showed Charlotte moving through the wooded lot behind Sinclair's property. He'd wait until she reached the road and likely a car before his team would depart to follow.

Each flash of the dot tracking Charlotte felt like a heartbeat. His connection to her was stronger than a satellite signal. What would that mean for them after his assignment was complete? Charlotte might not feel the same. She could be happy for their work partnership to end, mission complete, and see him board a plane for home. But he wouldn't be satisfied leaving on those terms.

"Let me know when you want to go," the driver of the car said.

"Give them a little more time." Without warning, the tracking dots disappeared from the computer screen. His breath caught in his throat. He held up his handheld radio to his mouth. "What's going on? I lost the GPS signal."

"So did the computers in the command room. Hold positions until we can bring the signals back on line."

Austin pounded the car window and shouted in frustration. The GPS trackers were his only link to Charlotte. "Go," he ordered the driver. "I'm not sitting here while they get away."

Fifteen minutes later, Austin's anger boiled over. The GPS signal hadn't been recovered. The street that bordered the woods of Charlotte's last-known location was empty of people and vehicles. Had Robert found the trackers on her and destroyed them? Austin had been foolish to think they could outsmart the Presque Killer. He pictured Charlotte, bound and afraid. Then another image appeared in his mind. Charlotte Reid was a fighter. Maybe Robert had outmaneuvered everyone else but Austin believed the killer wouldn't outsmart Charlotte.

Please God, stay with her and give her strength and wisdom. Austin continued to pray.

Charlotte's awareness slowly returned. Her mind felt foggy. It took almost a minute to remember what happened or where she was. Or more specifically, who she was with. A deafening roar drowned out all other noises. She blinked her eyes open and gazed up at the night sky moving quickly above. The smell of murky water and moss and the whirring noise of fan blades informed her that she was on an airboat, gliding through the bayou. High above in the heavens, stars twinkled and the waxing moon shone bright. *Guide Austin to me.*

She attempted to move. Her body was wrapped tight in some sort of blanket. With every effort to free herself, she produced a crinkling sound. She tipped her chin to try and view what bound her. The shine off the silver metallic blankets confused her initially. The air temperature remained warm all night, so why would he secure her in emergency warming blankets? She looked like a gas station burrito, which would have made her laugh under any other circumstance.

The reason for the blankets struck her so hard she gasped. The metal on the blankets wasn't to keep her warm. It was to block any GPS signals. The moment Robert wrapped her entire body, from neck to shoes, in these blankets, the trackers must've stopped providing Austin and the rescue team with her location. She was left on her own with a killer.

Charlotte struggled to free herself. The cord wrapped around her body held tight. Robert was taking her somewhere in the bayou. She hoped he'd bring her to the place he was keeping the other women. Once they arrived, she must free herself and his captives. No one was coming to save them.

She glanced over at Robert, seated up by the giant fan propeller in the back, smiling with his success. He'd outsmarted everyone once again. Or at least that was what he thought.

They'd placed three GPS trackers on her. The one in her jacket pocket and jeans pocket were stuck under the blanket. She had no freedom of movement to get them out. But her shoe. She might be able to slip it off her foot. Would

Robert question if she were shoeless when they arrived at their destination?

The warming blanket around her feet was wrapped loosely. Charlotte moved her feet back and forth in small kicks to produce an opening in the folds of the blanket. The tracker was inside the sole of her left shoe. And although she could stick out her shoe and leave it on, she worried Robert would wrap up her feet again or have another trick at their destination to block the signal.

Using the sole of her right shoe, she pushed down on the left heel. She had never been one to tie her laces tight, and after a short while, her left shoe slipped off her foot. She shoved it out from under the protection of the blanket through the opening she'd made earlier. With her heart racing, she slipped off the right shoe and then forced it out to join its mate. Now both feet were shoeless, and she prayed Robert would be too distracted to notice her stocking feet.

One GPS tracker now had an unobstructed line up into the sky. For how long? Hopefully long enough for the boat to reach its destination, providing Austin with her location.

The sound of the propellers quieted and the boat slowed. It passed underneath thick tree branches draped with Spanish moss. In the dark, they looked like skeletons wearing ragged clothing. The moonlight that had provided comfort had been replaced by spooky shadows. They traveled slowly, creeping along past bald cypresses standing majestically over their swampy dominion.

The boat glided to a stop, bumping into a solid surface.

"Welcome, Detective. I've been anticipating having you as a guest." Robert's voice blended with the deafening sounds of the croaking of bull frogs and droning insects. He hauled her up with surprising strength. Once she was upright, he climbed on the dock and pulled her up with him.

She could barely keep her balance. Her movement was so restricted by what she now saw as red nylon cording. Being pulled along by Robert, she waddled across the short dock then onto the front porch of a shack that had seen better days. These types of buildings had been built as fishing and hunting lodges, and for men to come out into the swamp and drink while escaping their families. Often the shacks, which were poorly built on wood pylons, fell into disrepair and were taken back by the bayou. The one that Robert had taken her to appeared to be on a similar route.

Robert stopped by the front door of the run-down stilt house. He pointed to the porch covering. "Metal roofing. If you got anything on you that's sending a tracking signal, it's not getting through the metal sheets covering the roof." His fingers worked to untie the cord. He unwrapped her, then tossed the balled-up emergency blankets on the porch. He reused the cord to tie Charlotte's wrists behind her back and then to secure her ankles.

Although she wanted to struggle, the drugs he'd given her hadn't fully left her system. Her muscles felt weak, and her brain remained foggy. She fought the urge to glance at the boat to make sure her shoe was still inside. The trees might weaken the GPS signal but it would have a better chance at reaching Austin than on her foot as she was led into the house.

Her gazed scanned the dark interior, searching for other signs of life. "Where are the others?" They had to be here. They had to still be alive.

"The reunion will commence shortly." Robert gripped her arm and guided her to a metal kitchen chair. "Take a seat and get comfortable." He made quick work of tying Charlotte to the chair.

She strained against her bonds but the cord wouldn't

give. "I remember you, Bobby. I found a picture of us with our parents and Ruby. How did you end up like this? A cold-blooded killer. You stole Ruby from me." Grief and rage blended together, creating a storm inside her. Looking into Robert's cold, emotionless eyes, Charlotte couldn't believe he was the same man she'd spoken with at church less than a week ago. Or that he was the same little boy who'd hidden from his father in her and Ruby's bedroom.

"I'm pleased your memory has been jogged. I can't begin to explain how distressing it is to see someone again, someone who you felt so close to at one time in your life, who does not recall your name." Robert pushed back the curtain covering a window and gazed outside. No light filtered through the dirty glass pane. He let the curtain fall back into place, then reached for a lantern hanging on a long nail set in the wall. After a few clicks, the room was illuminated by the glow of the propane lantern. Robert held the lantern up to his face. "Charlotte and Ruby, the inseparable sisters. You always looked out for each other."

"Until you killed Ruby," she hissed. "Why? Help me to understand why you kill? Why you wanted me to be the one to try to stop you?"

His sinister laugh bounced off the tight walls. "Your question only shows how little you understand of human nature. How little you cared about anyone else besides yourself and your sister. My days with you were a blip in your timeline. For me, they were the only bright spot of my childhood."

"Help me understand." A plea meant to buy time. She wasn't sure how long they'd been traveling before she woke up in the boat, but once Austin got a GPS signal of her location, it would take him a while to reach her.

Robert pulled out chair matching the one Charlotte was

tied to, and dragged it over. The metal feet scraped across the raw plank flooring. He sat, feet spread, elbows on his knees, so his face was only inches away. "When I moved into your house, I thought I'd won the lottery. My mom had taken off before I was out of diapers. Your mom was so kind and loving. You look just like her, you know. She had a kind heart, unlike her daughters."

"Ruby and I didn't mean to exclude you. Our mom had people coming in and out of our lives all the time. We didn't grow attached to anyone." A manual clock hung on the wall. The ticking of the second hand boomed in Charlotte's ears. Ten minutes until midnight.

"I was only looking for a friend." His warm breath smelled foul.

She almost gagged. "I had a rough childhood too. Ruby and I went into foster care shortly after you and your dad moved out. Then our mom died in prison. I didn't grow up to be a serial killer."

"No. You became a police officer. Respected in the community. Unlike Ruby, who became a disgrace. But in actuality, I felt sympathy for her. She had to try and live up to a big sister who could do no wrong." He shook his head. "Ruby cried out for you to save her. How does that make you feel, Charlotte, to know your sister was looking for you and you never came?"

Charlotte burned with rage and stretched the cord around her wrists, trying to break free. All thought of the ongoing rescue operation had been replaced with the need to wipe that disgusting smile off Robert's face. Her bonds held no matter how she fought.

Rational thinking returned, and she stilled. Austin and his team needed more time. She had to keep Robert talking. Soon, the man known as the Presque Killer would prepare to take more lives, including her own. Would he strangle her like he did the others? What would her final thoughts be right at the end?

No. She had to fight. Good had to win.

NINETEEN

"It's time for you to meet my other guests." Robert stood and kicked back his chair, sending it tumbling to the ground.

She instinctively recoiled, though her movement was restricted. At least he hadn't covered her mouth. "What brought you to this point, Robert? You've murdered five people, that we know of. And you want to add four more. There has to be a better way to deal with what you're feeling than killing."

"Somehow, I managed to survive childhood with only a few broken bones and emotional scars. For the most part I was able to blend in. No matter how hard I tried to be normal, dying and death continued to fascinate me. So I studied biology and pathology. Dealing with the dead during an autopsy satisfied my curiosity. Then, seven years ago, I traveled to Presque to attend the jazz festival." While he spoke, Robert wound and unwound a two-foot section of red cord around his left hand.

Charlotte imagined the feeling of the cord around her neck. *Hurry, Austin.*

"Do you recall me coming up to you after the first band finished their set?" He stared down at her through narrowed eyes. "Of course you don't. I tried to talk with you but you barely looked at me."

"I'm sorry. I should have remembered you. To be honest, I blocked out much of that time with my mom. It's too painful for me to relive those years." Perhaps reminding him again that her childhood had left scars too.

"I saw you still wore that gold bracelet with the crescent moon." He continued talking as if she hadn't spoken. "A rage filled me. Ruby always had your love. Back when we were children and as adults. Not me. You acted like you cared about me but you never did. Not like you did Ruby. I thought if I snuff out the lives of women who looked like you, I'd feel at peace. Then I figured if I took away the one person you love, I'd be vindicated. And it worked, for a little while."

"You found a love of your own." The sick, twisted man standing before her wasn't worthy of love. He'd acted like a God-fearing man to trick a woman into marrying him. "Vanessa is pregnant. Robert, please don't hurt anyone else. Let us all go then turn yourself in. You're going to be a father."

"I never wanted that." His mouth twisted in a scowl. "Can you imagine me, responsible for raising another human being? I'm even worse than my own dad. I won't do to my kid what my dad did to me. No, Vanessa will be better off raising the kid alone." He lurched forward, untied Charlotte and dragged her to her feet. "It's finally midnight. You had more than enough time to stop me. I win. Let's go claim my prize."

She struggled against him as he yanked her toward a closed door at the back of the room. He swung open the door and shoved Charlotte inside. She landed hard on her knees, crying out in pain. An awful smell hit her, and she struggled to breathe the stale air. Then, she heard muffled cries.

When her eyes adjusted to the darkness of the room,

Charlotte stilled at the sight of three women seated and bound in chairs—Karen Tremont, Candy Lyon and Lisa Ann Benton. At seeing Charlotte, their cries increased.

"Who's going first?" Robert strode before the three women, letting his gaze linger on each. "You'll be last, Detective Charlotte Reid. I'm sure after all the years of chasing me, you'd like a chance to observe my work."

"Stop, Robert!" Despite the volume of her cry, her voice didn't register with Robert, who was too fixated on his selection.

"Let's begin with the one who's been trapped here the longest." He grabbed Karen by the hair and yanked back her head. Robert stared down into her terrified eyes. "Put her out of her misery."

Charlotte struggled to get back up on her feet. Compelled by the will to protect, she lurched forward, ready to fight to her last breath.

"Go faster," Austin yelled at the airboat driver. "We're almost there." His gaze had barely left his laptop screen since the GPS signal had been restored. He'd almost kissed that flashing blue dot when it reappeared. Those with better knowledge of the area than Austin informed the team that Robert had taken Charlotte into a bayou approximately fifteen miles south of town.

Austin had never moved so fast or yelled commands so loudly. Within minutes, they'd been speeding to the nearest landing. A group of airboats and drivers had been assembled on short notice, showing the resolve of the community to capture the man who'd terrorized them for too long.

The loss of the GPS signal had brought him to his knees. He'd raged they wouldn't be able to locate Charlotte or the kidnapping victims before it was too late. Now he was about a mile away from the source of the last remaining signal they tracked. He prayed it would lead him to Charlotte's location and not a spot where Robert had dumped a tracker. The number shown on the computer screen matched the number to the tracker he'd put inside her shoe. Robert might have found and disposed of the others but a tracker hidden inside the sole of a tennis shoe would be more difficult to find.

Without warning, all boat propellers were silenced. "We're close now," the driver of his airboat said. "Don't want to advertise we're coming. Grab an oar and quietly start rowing."

Austin, along with a member of the SWAT team, did as instructed. The boat glided over the water in the direction the driver indicated. Soon, they entered a forest growing out of the water. A bird cried overhead. Something splashed in the dark water nearby. A shadow of a large object hovering above the water's surface appeared. When the boat grew closer, he recognized the shape as a house built on stilts. It appeared to have been built many years ago and the next strong storm could blow it over.

Weak light spilled out the two windows at the front of the house. Besides the sounds of animals and insects, all was quiet and still.

Once his boat connected with the rickety dock attached to the house, Austin hopped up and out. He removed his gun from the holster and switched off the safety. Five members of the SWAT team joined Austin on the deck and unholstered their weapons. Three others remained behind a boat in case the suspect fled.

He gazed down into Robert's airboat and noticed Charlotte's shoes lying on the bottom. Smart. The metal roof of the house would block GPS signals coming from inside. Austin checked his emotions, which had bubbled up and spilled over like a pot of boiling water. Right now, he needed a clear head. After years of keeping a tight lid on his feelings, the possibility of losing Charlotte had turned up the heat. He couldn't bear the thought of facing a future without her. He loved her. She'd altered his life's goals. He needed Charlotte's light to escape the dark.

"There are four female victims being held inside," he whispered. "Only fire your weapon as a last resort."

After getting a visual confirmation each team member was ready, Austin crept to the door and gave the hand signal to breach. As they moved in, he prayed they weren't too late.

Charlotte had tried and failed. She'd been restrained again, tied up so tightly to a kitchen chair that she could barely breathe. Tears spilled down her face.

Robert, positioned behind Karen, wrapped a strand of red cord around her neck. "Quiet now. It will all be over soon."

A crash sounded from the front room, making them all jump.

"Robert Sinclair," a man shouted. "Surrender. You're under arrest."

"Austin," Charlotte cried out through the gag covering her mouth. He'd come. He'd found her.

Robert released the red cord and searched the room for an escape. His eyes looked wild, like those of a trapped animal.

Austin burst into the room. He rushed to Charlotte and pulled down the gag on her mouth. "Are you all right?"

"He's getting away." While she appreciated his concern, capturing the Presque Killer was the priority.

An enraged scream sounded as Robert ran toward an open window.

"Stop!" Austin rushed forward, gun drawn.

Robert produced a gun of his own from the waist of his jeans, pointed and fired at Austin.

Fortunately, the bulled missed, striking the wall. All four women, including Charlotte, cried out.

In response, Austin took a shot, which struck Robert in the leg as he was fleeing through the window opening.

Robert fell and splashed into the water below.

Soon, a boat floated to the rear of the house and gave a brief chase. Robert, who was swimming, didn't stand a chance. "We got him," a SWAT team member yelled.

"Is he really captured?" Charlotte shook out her hands after one of the men who'd arrived with Austin untied the cord around her wrists. Once her body was freed, she rushed to the window. Below, she saw an airboat with three men dressed in black with rifles strapped to their backs and headlamps glowing on their heads. The boat also carried the driver and one other passenger, who appeared to be treating Robert's nonlethal gunshot wound. A feral-looking Robert Sinclair lay surrounded on the bottom of the boat, soaking wet, with no chance of escape.

Charlotte removed her gaze from Robert to the three women in the room who were standing, free. Charlotte hugged each of them, then guided the women outside and into an airboat that would take them home. She watched the boat disappear into the darkness, and her legs began trembling. She grabbed a post to hold herself steady.

A strong arm wrapped around her waist and pulled her close. She leaned into Austin's strength. Every ounce of her own had been drained. She peered up at him. He looked uncharacteristically disheveled. His tousled dark hair complemented the stubble covering his lower face. Before heading out on the mission, he'd changed out of his usual dress clothes into black cargo pants and a black long-sleeved shirt covered with a bulletproof vest. Admittedly, she loved this rugged tactical look as much as his suave FBI special agent persona.

"It's over." He stared out into the distance. "Robert is being taken directly to jail."

"It's really over." The possibility seemed unreal. "He blames me for his need to murder. He killed Ruby as revenge for me loving my sister but not himself as a brother." Her chest tightened. Would she ever fully process the information Robert had provided? "He came up to me at the jazz festival seven years ago and I didn't remember him." Pain seared her heart. "If only I had remembered, all those he murdered would still be alive."

"Don't play that game." Austin held her upper arms and met her gaze. "A serial killer like Robert would have acted the same under different circumstances. It's not your fault he fixated on you."

She tried to shake out of his hold but his grip held firm. Charlotte wanted to run away and hide forever. How could she face the rest of her life haunted by Robert's actions? She'd jump in the water and swim away if she weren't so fearful of the murky water filled with alligators.

"Three women are alive today due to your bravery, Charlotte." He gave her a little shake to regain her attention. "You saved those women. If you hadn't allowed yourself to be captured, he would have killed them."

His words sank in. Karen, Candy and Lisa Ann were free. They'd survived. Because Charlotte had faced a monster. "Well, you and your team saved the day."

One side of his mouth lifted. "You probably want your

shoes back. How did he manage to block the GPS signal until you reached here?"

She pointed to the emergency blankets tossed in the corner of the porch. "He's smart, I'll give him that. But I'm smarter."

"Yes, you are." Austin kissed the top of her head.

Love for this wonderful man burst inside her. No use denying the obvious. No more fighting the pull. God had placed them together again for a purpose. She understood His purpose was greater than anything she could have imagined. A yawn as deep and wide as the Grand Canyon escaped her mouth. "As soon as I know Robert is locked up, securely behind bars, I'm taking a shower then sleeping for days."

"I can get behind that. Do you mind waiting until the crime scene techs and Chief Gunther arrive? Chief offered to be in charge of this crime scene so I can get you home."

Home. She pondered the reality of going home. With the killer caught, Austin would leave soon. On to his next assignment. And what about Charlotte? What came next for her life? Had the events surrounding the Presque Killer drained her to the level she had nothing left for law enforcement? Only time would tell.

She had a few more days with Austin. Then she'd once again say goodbye. Finally, she understood his commitment to his job didn't exclude him from a romantic relationship. Not when she was willing to sacrifice to make a relationship with him work. He'd need to fully let down his emotional guard, which she noticed had slipped more and more over their week working together.

The last time he'd left Presque, she'd allowed hurt to spill over into anger. She couldn't allow others to dictate her actions. To capture the Presque Killer, she'd stopped playing the killer's game and devised her own strategy. When facing her fears, she'd switched from defense to offense. Now she needed to take the initiative again in order to succeed at love.

TWENTY

Two days later, Austin knocked on Charlotte's front door. His packed suitcase waited inside the SUV. He was leaving for Baton Rouge. His flight left in four hours. But he wasn't ready to say goodbye.

Since the night in the bayou when they'd arrested Robert Sinclair, he'd been caught in a whirlwind of activity. Statements were given. He'd traveled back to the bayou shack to walk through the scene for his report to the FBI. Charlotte had been busy as well, and he'd barely spent more than a few minutes alone with her.

He'd texted her, saying he was coming over. So she should be home. He knocked again. A moment later, the door swung open.

"I'm sorry." Charlotte stood at the screen door, waving him inside. "I was on the phone with Chief Gunther. He's extending my leave to six weeks."

"How do you feel about that?" He hoped she'd use the time to take a vacation. Rest and relax. Leave the trauma behind for a while.

She padded with bare feet through the front room and into the kitchen. "I'm not sure how I feel about being benched for six weeks. Part of me is relieved. I don't have a clear head for investigative work."

"Are you considering a career change?" He accepted a glass of lemonade from Charlotte. Last night, he'd typed his resignation letter to the FBI. While racing through the bayou to rescue Charlotte, not knowing if she was alive or dead, he'd concluded he couldn't continue keeping his heart separate from his work. When he let in all the suppressed emotions, Austin had been left with a clear vision of his future. He knew Caleb, who'd loved Austin like a son, would approve.

"I may decide to leave law enforcement. I'm not sure yet." She shrugged. "I guess that's what these six weeks are partially for." After setting her glass of lemonade down on the counter, she took a deep breath and strode toward him. When she reached him, Charlotte pressed her hand to her heart. "I do know that I don't want you to leave before I lose the nerve to do this." She lifted up on her tiptoes and brushed her lips against his.

The connection felt as light as a feather and struck him with the force of a hurricane.

"I didn't want you to leave before I told you that I love you, Special Agent Austin Walsh." She grinned. "You are a true partner in every sense of the world. Whatever comes next for me and for you, I want you in my life. Maybe with a little less logic and a little more room for love?"

She loved him. His body felt lighter than air. This farewell was an improvement over the last time he'd left. Austin swept her up in his arms. "I've made the decision to end my career chasing criminal and killers. By the time my mentor left the Bureau, he'd waited too long. Caleb was burned out to the point he never recovered. His daughter had been murdered and he'd made it his mission to hunt serial killers. Caleb's mission became mine." The image of Caleb lying in a hospital bed, hooked up to monitors and tubes often came to mind. Caleb had trusted Austin to take over the work of bringing serial killers to justice. But after years of doing just that, he felt his heart move in a different direction.

"Leave the FBI?" Charlotte's eyes widened. "Your work makes a real difference. You save lives."

"I still want to change the world, just go about it a little differently." For the last two years, he'd been putting together a project that would identify youth with psychological tendencies corresponding with a potential serial killer and attempt to change their outcomes through intervention. "I need to go back to Virginia to collect my belongings, but I'm coming back to Presque."

"You're not needed to testify until the trial begins, which will be a while."

"You said you love me, right? Or did my ears play a trick on me?"

She nodded and wrapped her arms around his waist. "I did and I do."

"I love you too." He kissed the tip of her nose. "I'm returning soon because I don't want to be away from you any more than I have to. I want to take you out on a date, with good food and wine and no talk of murders or killers."

"I'd really like that," she said with a laugh. "So tell me about this different path you see yourself on. Is there room for me to travel alongside you? Another partnership, perhaps?"

"My darling Charlotte." He leaned in for another kiss. "I wouldn't want it any other way."

* * * * *